THE LAST REFUGEE

Zahara Schara

Cover design by: Zahara Schara

To the amazing women in my life.
Jacqueline, Sabrina, Elizabeth and Mabel.

CONTENTS

THE LAST
REFUGEE

THE BUNNY

Present day

E li was old; he knew that. When exactly it had happened he wasn't too sure, but he was indeed old, set in his ways.

He would start his morning with toast and coffee, a habit he had adopted when he lived on a kibbutz. He liked quiet mornings so, in order to avoid the communal dinning hall, he bought a tiny toaster and some instant coffee. He still liked the quiet of the morning. Someone once told him: if you are quiet in the morning, you can decide how your day will be without any further influence. As he sat on the small patio, overlooking his vast but tidy garden, he noticed that the carrots had been plucked from the ground.

"Damn," he muttered.

Eli, barefoot with his cup of coffee in hand, stepped on the dew-laden grass to investigate further. Sure enough, each carrot had been unceremoniously torn from its spot, well before they would have been fully matured.

He then walked slowly around the perimeter of his wood fence, looking for the hole the rabbits had made. But he saw no hole. And despite being old, he knew that there had indeed been carrots there the day before.

After his coffee, he spent hours tending to his garden. The garden filled nearly all of his backyard, and produced more vegetables than he could consume himself. So, depending on the season, his neighbors would receive bushels of strawberries or tomatoes, or even the occasional bouquet of roses or lilacs. His wife had loved the flowers and, while he didn't cultivate them anymore, he couldn't bring himself to cut down what still remained. He tended to the bushes dutifully.

His day would usually be followed by a trip to the market, a stop in the local cafe and perhaps a game of chess with his old friend James.

Eli was flustered. When he reached the cafe, he dropped his hat on the chair and, before even ordering a drink or greeting his friend, stated, "A rabbit is going to destroy my garden."

James merely raised an eyebrow to this. The number of Eli's rants had increased with his age, as if his temperament was regressing rather than aging along with him. James did not look up or interject, knowing that

2

this was merely the beginning.

"Damn thing, took every last carrot."

James took the liberty of ordering for Eli. It was the same every day: one shot of espresso. He began to set up the chess board as Eli ranted on.

"I've searched the perimeter and I can't find where it is getting in."

"I have a hunting rifle you can borrow," James said, a little too enthusiastically.

"No, no," Eli said as he waved his hand at him, and continued, "But I must buy a trap. I'll be back." He stood to go, mindless of the espresso or the game they hadn't started.

Eli didn't have anything against hunting, but he had no intention of even eating rabbit, let alone killing one. So off he went in search of a rabbit trap.

At the hardware store, he was again offered the use of a rifle. Again, he declined the offer.

"Well, if you don't kill it, it will keep coming back," the clerk said in a condescending tone. When Eli turned and scowled at him, the young kid immediately regretted adding his two cents.

"If I capture it alive and then release it, it will show me where the hole in my fence is and I will be able to keep this from happening with another rabbit," he retorted.

The clerk's eyes widened; this thought had never occurred to him. Then, snapping back to the moment, he said, "I will have to order a trap. It will be here on Thursday. Are you sure you don't want the rifle in meantime?"

"Thank you, but I'll see you on Thursday."

Eli returned to the cafe where James had convinced the café owner's son to play chess with him. Eli sat down, drank his cold espresso and watched them play, whispering into the boy's ear what moves to make.

The youngster made a cautious move, and then almost inaudibly said "check".

"You are cheating!" James protested.

Eli laughed. "No, not cheating, educating."

***

Wednesday morning brought the surprise of missing lettuce. And Eli couldn't help but wonder, was it a family of rabbits or something bigger perhaps? A badger? A fox? But surely a hole for anything larger would be noticeable.

Thursday morning, he was waiting for the clerk before the store even opened.

"I would have shot the damn thing," the clerk said as he handed the trap to Eli.

"Then you'd be a fool," Eli said as he slid the money across the counter. The younger man rolled his eyes.

Eager to set up the trap, Eli returned home immediately, albeit with the knowledge that nothing would be captured in the daylight. Nonetheless, the trap was set before noon. Eli debated what to use as bait, changing his mind three times, and finally settling on a piece of bread smeared with Nutella.

Now, all he had to do was wait.

He woke up the next morning with the eagerness of a kid at Christmas, but peering from his kitchen window, he could see the trap was empty. Going outside to take a closer look only confirmed his suspicions, and he could also see that spinach was now missing too.

"Damn," he mumbled to himself—not that there was anyone to hear, but being married for forty-seven years had left with him the habit.

He changed the bait, figuring some apple slices might do the trick. He left the bread though, just in case.

Again, nothing happened.

By the third day, he was raving mad.

"I've left the thing a damn buffet!!" he swore at an unmoved James.

James nodded quietly, and went over to the coat

rack, where he retrieved his shotgun. Without saying a word, he handed it to Eli, looking more smug than he intended. From his pocket, he produced a box of shells.

Eli took them both without saying a word. He ordered an extra espresso and headed home. It was going to be a long night.

Eli cleared a spot in the kitchen so he had room for a chair, a small table and so he could prop the gun on the window seal. He only loaded one shell, knowing that he was an excellent marksmen and, despite the dark and his age, he'd only need one shot. The fact that James had given him an entire box felt like an insult.

Darkness came slow, as spring was turning into summer and it was nearly a full moon. Eli didn't move, his eyes fixed on the garden. He let his eyes adjust to the darkness. He had debated leaving another light on in the house, but it wouldn't illuminate as far as he needed to see.

He nodded off a few times, and had to shake himself awake. He drank coffee that had turned cold, but he didn't dare get up to make another for fear of making any noise. Around 3am, as he was nodding off again, something caught his eye. It wasn't coming from under his fence but from above.

At first, he thought it was a man, then perhaps a teenager, but as it got closer he realized that it was a small child. He took his finger from the trigger, leaned back in his seat and watched, his mind and his eyes not fully able to comprehend what he was seeing.

He remained still, to not give away his position. He watched as the child slowly knelt down and began pulling things from his garden indiscriminately. He felt his temper rise, but he steadied himself.

The child shoved a few handfuls of leafy greens into a plastic shopping bag, and stealthily climbed back over the fence.

As dawn approached, Eli sat there in silence, thinking about where the child must have come from. The nearest house was kilometers away, and Eli either had to bike or drive to town. This wasn't a teenage prankster but a very small child.

His heart sank as he realized that there was only one explanation for this: the child must be from the camp.

He referred to "the camp," as if there were only one in the world, but Eli knew there were more. A refugee camp on the outside of the city, built for 800 people but now occupied by thousands. But even so, it was over six kilometers away. Could a child that small make it in the dark, alone?

Eli was angry, very angry, yet he couldn't pinpoint the exact reason. His conscience was bothered and he couldn't settle it. He attempted to justify his own anger, assuring himself that stealing was stealing, or

convincing himself that it was cowardly adults sending a child, knowing there'd be no punishment they
were caught.

Yet, what bothered him more was in not knowing
what to do next. Eli emptied the gun, left it open on
the table and retreated to his bed, but his own mind
would not grant him reprieve.

The next day he returned the gun to James.

"Did you get the bastard? You look like shit."

Eli nodded and then walked out. It was only later that
James noticed there were no shells missing. He assumed the trap had worked after all.

Eli drove toward the coast, but then turned south and
headed toward Paris. It was a bad habit but one he
never could rid himself of. He always headed to Paris
when nothing else made sense.

PARIS

June 1942

"Wake up Eli," his mother whispered as she gently rubbed his back. The sun wasn't yet up, and the little boy rubbed his eyes. Sitting next to him, his mother smiled. Hannah was a beautiful woman, and not only in her son's eyes. Her features were dark, nearly exotic, with dark brown hair and emerald green eyes. Nothing like the blond curls that she pushed away from Eli's face.

"We are going on trip," she said, trying her best to sound excited.

"Can Louise come?" Eli asked.

"Of course Louise can come!" she said as she reached for the well-worn bunny that Eli held. The toy had been a gift from before he was born and had been named Louise. Louise has seen better days, which was clear to see by the amount of times she had been mended, usually with different color thread.

Hannah had done her best to prepare Eli for if this moment came. She told him of exciting far off places, with prince and princess. She told him of the Pyramids in Egypt and cowboys in America. Her husband told her that she was being overly anxious, that though things were bad, the allies would be there soon. If they could only wait a bit longer, things would go back to the way they were. This war couldn't last forever. And even if they did have to leave, where would they go?

Many nights, Eli had heard his parents arguing in hushed tones, at one time, joined by their upstairs neighbors. Eli couldn't figure out what all the commotion was about. But his vast life experience at five years old told him that something was being kept secret. He asked his best friend, Bernard, who lived upstairs and whose parents had been arguing with his. Bernard was ten, and therefore all-knowing in Eli's mind.

"Do you know the secret?" Eli had asked.

"Of course I do, stupid," Bernard scoffed.

Eli made a pouting face to show that he didn't like being called stupid, but he wasn't angry enough to walk away. He wanted to know what the secret was.

"It's about my birthday." Bernard beamed. "They must be planning a great surprise for me. And they know you are too much of baby to keep secrets." Bernard wasn't usually such a bully but today he wasn't on his own, and when other boys were around he was particularly nasty, repeatedly teasing Eli about his stuffed bunny which he brought everywhere. Often, Eli would run home in tears, and then would sit on his bed, hugging Louise and reassuring her that they didn't need any other friends.

"Is Bernard coming too?" Eli asked now, as he dressed in the clothes that his mother had laid out.

"No," Hannah answered, sharper than she had intended to, but she offered no further explanation. Her eyes then turned sad.

"But—" Eli began to inquire.

"It's an adventure for only you and me."

Eli was confused. Why was no one else coming? Especially daddy—he would love an adventure too.

"Then I am not going." He sat down and pulled his knees up to his chest.

Hannah had been doing her best to keep calm, with the hope of keeping Eli calm too. David and Hannah had agreed that it would be safer for the two of them to go first, so as not to raise any suspicions. As Jews, the last thing they wanted was to draw attention to themselves. These were scary times. They had stayed as long as they'd dared. Crossing to the south was more than dangerous; in David's eyes, it was suicidal. Knowing their best bet was for Hannah to bribe her way across, he had sold anything and everything that would fetch a price. He told her that he had split the money in half, for when he would cross, but he put the entire amount in her bag. He would find another way. More than anything, he wanted his wife and son to be safe.

Hannah and David had discussed their plans with their upstairs neighbors with the hopes that Sara and Bernard would join Hannah, with Charles following with David. But Charles refused; he would not allow his family to be separated for any reason.

"Whatever comes, we will face it together," he kept saying, his fingers intertwined with Sara's. Hannah knew that Sara didn't agree but also knew that it wasn't her place to say so.

"Maybe you should stay," David had later said to her sympathetically.

"You fool, we are Jews!" she hissed, not wanting to fight this fight again.

"They are only deporting the foreign Jews. We are French."

"And what do you think will happen when they run out of *them*? We'll be next. You know this. We have to leave."

David's family had been in France for more generations than anyone could have counted, but Hannah family had only been become naturalized citizens a few years ago. Her family had been in the Pale settlement. She didn't know if they would consider her and Eli to be "French," but she knew that they would definitely be considered Jews.

David sighed, knowing she was right. Things had only gotten worse since the occupation, and though he hoped they were close, they couldn't wait for the allies.

Hannah grabbed Eli's arm, and pulled him to his feet. Dragging him behind her, she moved through the house, carrying the small suitcase she had packed for them.

Eli tugged free and ran to David, crying at the top of his lungs. "No, I don't want to go!"

David embraced him. He looked at his wife sorrowfully.

"Be good, and listen to your mama," he told Eli, wiping away his tears and trying to calm the little boy who was almost beyond the point of consoling. "Be my brave adventurer, and write to tell me about all the wonderful things you and your mother see." Eli finally smiled at the thought of this.

Hannah and David embraced. He kissed her forehead.

"Please…" Hannah said, not finishing the rest of the sentence, but David knew everything she was asking.

He stood at the doorway as Hannah and Eli walked away, hand in hand, chatting merrily as if they were indeed going on a great adventure. He watched as they turned the corner, quietly closing the door and murmuring a prayer for their safety. He would follow in July, under the guise of taking a holiday by the sea.

Once they were out of their own neighborhood, Hannah reached down and ripped the star off of Eli's coat before doing the same to her own. She removed the tiny armband that she had made for Louise as well. David couldn't understand why she'd made a miniature one for the stuffed bunny, but she had informed him matter-of-factly: "Eli won't be scared if Louise wears one as well. He is too young to know how serious it is." She balled up the yellow material and stuffed it under a flower pot on a nearby stoop.

Hannah hoped that if she kept her pace and her eyes down no one would notice them; she would just be another woman with a suitcase and a little boy. In this instance, it was her unique disadvantage that she was remarkably beautiful; by nature, she gained the attention of every man she passed.

They were stopped several times, but she had the perfect lie.

"My husband was in the army. He was a deserter before the line fell," she would say with a sigh. "They shot him. Coward."

Invariably, the solider would shake his head, a signal

that he had bought the ruse, and she'd continue on.

"German men are so courageous and disciplined. Hopefully my son can learn a thing or two. Right, Captain?" She smiled, knowing that this man in particular, red-faced and overweight, would fall for the flattery.

The words repulsed her, as did the way the man reached out to stroke her cheek with the back of his hand. But time after time the story never failed, and thankfully, neither did her forged ID cards, which bared the names Sophie and Alexandre Delcroix.

She hoped that the stops would become less frequent when they got out of the city but, as they headed toward the Free-Zone, she had no idea what to expect. Surely, the guards couldn't be watching every kilometer of the demarcation line.

Eli remembered walking for days on end. In his young mind, he was sure they had traveled thousands of kilometers.

ALEPPO

2014

Ahmed loved his noisy house. He always smiled when he would hear laughter as he approached from the outside. He had been an only child, and while he never wanted for anything, he had always wanted siblings. So now that his home was filled with three healthy, albeit loud, children, he considered himself a very lucky man.

It was early evening and he made his way into the house, stepping over bikes and toys as he did so. Nadir, one his five-year-old twins, by far the more mischievous of the two, came running.
"Asma hit me and she is in trouble," he proclaimed triumphantly, clearly all too pleased to tattle on his sister.

Ahmed was slightly puzzled by this. Unlike her brother, Asma was a painfully shy little girl, the kind who would break into tears merely at the thought of being in trouble. One only needed to look at her sternly to punish her. While Ahmed would never condone violence, Asma must have had a reason to hit her brother.

Safia came to greet him, kissing him on the cheek. He took a moment to take in her beauty. She didn't age, he thought to himself, as he smoothed down his black hair that had started to grey at the temples.

"Asma hit Nadir ?" he asked puzzled.

Safia rolled her eyes. "Yes, but Nadir and Ali had ganged up on her and were pinching her." Ali was the son of their neighbor, who spent so much time with his children that the five-year-olds were often regarded as a trio. Ali was Nadir's partner in crime and Asma was their favorite target. "Poor child has welts all over. Finally, she'd had all she could and properly smacked Nadir." She let out an exasperated sigh.

Ahmed turned quickly to his son who was still standing next to him. The little boy scurried away.

"Where are the other two?"

"I sent Ali home. And Asma is in her room, just as Nadir is supposed to be." She called loudly to make sure Nadir had heard.

"I'll talk to them," he said as he rubbed her shoulder and reached down to kiss the head of the infant in her arms. "At least this one isn't old enough to cause trouble."

"Give it a week." She chuckled.

Ahmed found his two eldest children in his study, and tried to keep a serious face when they revealed more about the source of their squabbles: it was because Asma had refused to eat a worm, in order to prove how tough she was to Ali and Nadir.

"Well, did you and Ali eat a worm?" Ahmed asked Nadir.

"No," he replied sheepishly.

"Ah, then I guess you two aren't that tough either. It seems the only way to settle this is for you two boys to have worms for supper. I will let Ali's mother know." He moved as if to grab his phone.

Nadir immediately began to wail.

"Or you can apologize to your sister."

He mumbled out an apology, then Ahmed told them to go wash their hands before supper.

***

After dinner that night, when the kids had been put to bed, Safia sat laughing. "Worms for diner? Now I've heard everything."

Ahmed shrugged and laughed as well.

"That Nadir is going to give me grey hair before I am forty, and Asma, she is his pupil. She plays innocent but his mischievousness is rubbing off on her. The other day, while we were at the park, he told her to climb a tree, and the next thing I knew she was half way up it! I thought I was going to have to climb up there to get her."

"You went to the park?" Ahmed asked.

"I can't keep them in the house forever."

Ahmed rubbed his forehead, a telltale sign of stress. It has been a very troublesome few years, and as far as he could tell, there were no signs that it would end soon. A few years ago, in 2011, rumors of a civil war had begun to circulate in a quantity that foretold some truth, but as had happened with the Arab Spring, Ahmed thought it would disappear as quickly as it arrived.

At the time, it had looked as if he was correct: protests had occurred in January only, and they had been mostly peaceful and confined to the capital city of Damascus. But now, three years later, Ahmed knew of the abundance of wounded coming into the hospital where he worked. Earlier that morning, he had tried to piece together a man's skull—not even a man, really more of a boy at seventeen. Ahmed had been successful in saving his life, but there was no way the boy would ever walk or talk again.

"We need to consider leaving," Safia said. It was a conversation that had taken place dozens of times over the last three years. Many of their closest friends had left the city already, some for other parts of the country, and some leaving the country altogether.

The cosmopolitan life they all had loved so much was turning into a war zone. But it simply wasn't as simple as packing up and moving. The city was divided, and though the East had become a war zone, in the west, where Ahmed and his family lived and worked, life went on almost as normal.

"I can't leave. I am a doctor," Ahmed replied. He had used this argument before, and it was something his wife loved him for.

"Well, I am doctor too. And I think we should leave."

Safia had met Ahmed in their last year of medical school in Damascus. She had even done better than him on most tests. She was not only beautiful but smart. When Ahmed asked to marry her, she had initially refused—not because she didn't love him, but because she couldn't see herself as a wife or a mother. Despite the fact she had been studying obstetrics, she was not sure she wanted children herself.

Ahmed made it clear that he wanted whatever she wanted, but still she'd hesitated. She had eventually agreed, but under one condition: that they wouldn't marry until they both graduated medical school. The day after they both graduated, they were married.

He took a position in cardiac surgery, while she started in obstetrics and pediatrics. Despite her own views on her future as a mother, Safia loved babies, and the couple were living the best life they could in Damascus. They had plenty of friends in the city, and though they were both busy doing residencies, they still made time for getaways and fancy dinners.

It was at one such dinner that Safia told Ahmed she had changed her mind and now wanted children, of course if he was open to the idea. Ahmed had hoped for this but had never pushed her.

The children were a long time in coming. First a year passed, then two, then three, but she did not become pregnant. Being around infants all day did little to help her mood, and Ahmed encouraged Safia to perhaps go into private practice. She refused, her reason that being around the children, helping to bring them into the world safety, was the next best thing.

Finally, after two rounds of IVF, Safia was pregnant, with twins no less. In 2009, at the age of thirty-five, she had Nadir and Asma via c-section. She didn't know it at the time, but the way they were born would become indicative of the personalities they would have for the rest of their lives. Nadir came into the world howling and kicking—even the doctor remarked on what a "strong set of lungs" he had. Asma, on the other hand, who was born second, was lifted out of her and didn't make a sound, instantly curling her body inward as she was taken from the comfort of what had been her home. It was terrifying for Safia when she didn't hear her cry, even after they announced the second baby was out. The doctor had to flick the bottom of her foot several times before she let out a soft cry.

Being a doctor of pediatrics had not prepared Safia for the enormity of having twins. Three days after bringing the babies home, she sat on the edge of the bed and wept. She kept mumbling, "I can't do this." Ahmed had watched in panic. He had tried to be helpful but it seemed everything he was doing was only making things worse. So he did the best thing he could think of in that moment: he phoned his mother and then Safia's aunt, the woman who had all but raised her. Within an hour, both were there, buzzing around the house, cooking, doing laundry, cradling the babies and assuring Safia that it would become easier.

They were right; it did become easier, but nonetheless, Safia and Ahmed agreed to wait longer before trying for another child. They wanted to space them apart. But as time passed, they came to the decision that they were content as a family of four. Both she and Ahmed had assumed that, because of the immense difficulty in conceiving the twins, they would need to use IVF again. But clearly, they were wrong. While a civil war waged, Salim was born in the summer of 2014. It was an immense surprise for them, with Safia being thirty-nine by this time.

Salim was born on a beautiful June day, with a mop of curly jet black hair. Compared to the twins, he was an easy baby. And despite having a newborn and two five-year-olds, Safia had finally hit her stride.

After the twins were born, Ahmed had been selected for a cardiac surgery fellowship in Aleppo. It would mean more time spent away from his young family, but Safia encouraged it, and eagerly moved the family from Damascus to Aleppo. They made they city their home and with the help of a nanny Safia went back to work, albeit part time.

In 2012, before Salim was born, Safia had floated the idea of sending her and the twins back to Damascus to stay with Ahmed's family, but his mother had been ill and Safia didn't want to separate the family. Safia thought it best to let the "troubles" as she called it blow over. And for a while it seemed as if she was right; there were small pockets of fighting over the next few months, but the family felt far removed from it. They'd continued about their daily lives, and at first, the changes, while an inconvenience, were manageable.

In February 2012, there were two suicide bombings that killed twenty-eight people and wounded hundreds more. In March, the private school the twins attended sent home a letter stating that since the safety of the children was their top priority, they would be stopping classes until further notice. The family, as did the entire city, held their breath and waited for whatever was to come next. Though Ahmed and Safia had tried to shield the children from as much as they could, the children could sense the obvious tension in the air.

The following year, the peace the family longed for did not come. In April, the city's most famed mosque was the victim of fighting between government forces and rebels, its thousand-year-old minaret brought collapsing to the ground after having been struck. The city was divided in two: the east was controlled by the opposition and the west by Assad government forces. In December, the idea that they could ride out the worst and wait for a resolution was shattered when the Syrian Air Force spent three days bombing in Aleppo. At least sixteen neighborhoods were hit and hundreds of civilians died. Ahmed did what he could, both at the hospital and at home, but any hopes of it "blowing over" were gone. That was also the time Safia was put on strict bedrest for what would prove to be a difficult pregnancy with Salim. The discussion of leaving the city had to be postponed. They'd remained thankful that they were in the western part of the city.

And then, for a while, there was an uneasy peace in the city. In 2014, while the rebels spent their energy and resources on fighting Isis, the government seized the chance, and it looked like all of Aleppo would be cleared. Ahmed and Safia, who didn't consider themselves to be politically involved, hoped this would be successful so that peace could return, but this hope once again proved futile when in May 2014, rebels blew up a hotel that was being used as command center for government forces. Retaliation was swift and barrel bombs once again began to fall.

While Ahmed was a brilliant heart surgeon, most of his days were spent tending to burns, gunshot wounds and removing shrapnel. He would jump in wherever he was needed, and it never became easier seeing how young most of the fighters were.

Salim was fast asleep in Safia's arms as she and Ahmed discussed leaving once more.

It's noble wanting to stay to help, but if we stay, we put the lives of our children at risk. You need to decide if it is worth it."

Ahmed knew she was right. In fact, he had thought as much in November even before the bombings. For a moment, he had considered returning to the capital, but his mother had passed in January, meaning there was nowhere for them to go, with no family left in Damascus. Word from his former medical school friends painted a similar picture of the violence occurring in Homs. Not only would they have to leave a beleaguered city, but they would have to travel much further to escape the devastation, leaving their beloved country behind as well.

They insisted that, wherever they go, they would do so as a family, but visas were hard to come by. Moving one person legally when the entire country seemed to be fleeing was hard enough; to move a family of five felt impossible. They felt trapped, like the millions of others who only wanted peace.

They both began looking for positions that would

sponsor visas. As accomplished doctors, they were sure that they would find something. They sent applications to Australia, Germany, England, the United States and South Africa. As a family, they endured what they could, while waiting and hoping.

THE ROAD SOUTH

Summer 1942

Hannah and Eli had made it far enough south to cross the demarcation line into Vichy, France. Hannah felt ill. She would have to steady her nerves, she told herself. She had procured passes the way anyone did in a time of war: she'd met an oily counterfeiter who assured her that he had spent years during the Spanish civil war perfecting his trade. This did little to comfort her. Everything about the man made her shift uncomfortably: the way he sucked on his teeth, his filthy appearance and the way he hissed the word "Jews" under his breath. Hannah had not offered up this information, but figured it must be obvious as one of the reasons why a woman and young child would be trying to pass the dangerous crossing alone.

While their forged documents had been good enough to make it this far, additional papers were needed to cross into the Free Zone legally, and this was the only way Hannah could think to get them. Trying to cross the border without papers was dangerous, and Hannah feared that if she and Eli were stopped, none of their falsified documents would hold up to any scrutiny. When she went to pick up the papers, she looked over her shoulder half a dozen times before knocking on the hotel room door. When the door opened, to Hannah's surprise, a young woman appeared on the other side. Without exchanging words, the woman hurried past Hannah, dragging with her a little girl whose little feet couldn't quite keep pace with that of her mother's. Hannah froze for a moment, till she heard the counterfeiter call out to her: "shut the damn door."

He dangled the documents in front of her and then demanded another twenty-five percent of what they had agreed. She threw the money down, snatched the papers out of his hand and swiftly disappeared before he could ask for anything else. She was glad she had left Eli asleep in the room she had rented.

Something in her gut told her not to trust this man, but looking over the papers, she didn't spot any glaring mistakes. She knew it was easy for a counterfeiter to sell documents that were easy to spot as false, and by the time the person realized they had been tricked, they were in far more danger. Eli was also only five, possibly the worst age to be in this situation. He was old enough to speak, but not yet old enough to grasp the danger of the truth. If separated from Hannah, Eli would become afraid and cry out for his father. Pressed hard enough, Eli might spill the entire truth. Either way, they would try to cross into the free zone the next morning. Hannah had stayed awake all night rolling the scenarios through her mind. She willed herself to sleep but it wouldn't come.

She dressed them both in silence. Eli could sense something was going on but he didn't ask. Hannah had hoped that if they crossed moments before sunrise, both the early hour and the fatigue of the soldiers manning the checkpoint would act in her favor. To her surprise, when she walked toward the checkpoint, she saw the same woman with the little girl directly in front of them. Hannah pulled back on Eli's hand, sensing something was not right. She moved to one side of the road, far enough to see the checkpoint but much harder to be seen herself due to the curve in the road. She watched the woman and little girl, she heard the screaming in German and what she thought was the word "liar." The woman grabbed the child, shoved the solider aside and took off running. Hannah cursed under her breath. She saw the quick flash of the guns against the darkness and then the woman and child lying like broken puppets on the street. She quickly gathered herself and Eli, and headed back toward town hastily. They would not be crossing today, or ever. Hannah knew the papers she had been sold were no good, but by the time they made it back to the hotel, the man was gone.

This part of the country was small, and rural, and outsiders stuck out no matter how inconspicuous they tried to be. The counterfeiter had taken most of their money, so Hannah knew they couldn't make it back to Paris safely. They went back to their small rented room to try to figure out what to do next. She felt so stupid for trusting a stranger, and the memory of the mother and child being shot replayed over and over again in her head.

"I'm hungry," Eli said.

These had been his first words of the day so far. Hannah hoped that being slightly behind her, he hadn't witnessed what she had, though she knew he had undoubtedly heard the shots. Hannah gathered him up and promised him a sweet breakfast as soon as the patisserie downstairs opened.

The next morning, they set off early. Where they were going, she wasn't sure. She wanted to get away from the border, from the memory of what could have been. Why did the woman run? Hannah kept wondering about what would she have done in that situation. The thought lingered in her mind.

They had been walking for hours and hours when she heard the sound of children laughing. Looking across a small field, she saw maybe twelve children chasing after a ball cheerfully. Eli begged her to let him go play, despite the fact that only a few minutes earlier he had been insisting he couldn't walk any further.

Hesitantly, she agreed, and Eli sprinted off toward the children.

Nearby, a large church loomed over its surroundings. She made her way to the stairs, sitting down to rest her feet and to watch Eli play. She couldn't remember the last time she had heard him laugh, she thought sadly.

She was totally engrossed in watching the children play that she didn't notice someone behind, not until they sat directly next to her. Hannah flinched, her reflexes still on edge, but a kindly nun patted her leg.

"I didn't mean to startle you." She smiled.

The woman was not beautiful, not in any traditional sense. She was of average build, had a slightly crooked smile and, under her habit, Hannah would have guessed she had mousey brown hair. Only the right side of her face seemed to move when she smiled. But her grey-blue eyes were comforting and warm.

Knowing she had nothing to fear from this woman, Hannah finally let a breath escape, unaware she had been holding it in.

"How old is he?" the nun asked, gesturing toward Eli.

"Five."

"Come inside and have some water," the nun said, rising from her seat. Seeing the panicked look in Hannah's eyes, she reassured her. "He will be fine with the other children."

Hannah followed the nun, stepping inside the cool dark church to a small but efficient kitchen toward the back. She finally introduced herself as sister Mary Joan. Hannah replied, giving their names as Sophie and Alexandre Delcroix and explaining that they were from a nearby village.

Sister Mary Joan raised an eyebrow and then leaned in, whispering to Hannah. "I don't need the whole truth—in fact it's probably better—but you are Jews, right?"

Hannah nodded slowly.

"Alright," Sister Mary Joan said in tone that made everything seem settled.

Hannah eyed her suspiciously, unsure of what was happening.

"I only have one rule." She looked Hannah squarely in the eye. "You cannot come back to visit or hang about. We can't draw any extra attention."

"I'm sorry, I am confused." Hannah managed to stumble through her words.

The nun looked her over, taking a step back and slowly saying, "You are here to leave the child with us, correct? Here, at the orphanage. We have three other children who are also Jews."

Hannah had never for a single moment considered

being separated from Eli. It seemed the worst possible option. What good was fleeing Paris if she and Eli and David were apart?

"We are waiting for my husband to join us from Paris. He is going to leave the first week of August."

Sister Mary Joan sat down and reached for Hannah's hand. "My dear, they began rounding up all the Jews in Paris two days ago. If he wasn't already on his way, I doubt he will be joining you anytime soon."

Hannah began to tremble as she thought about the idea of David being "rounded up". She replayed the scene from the checkpoint in her head again. She knew she and Eli were all but destitute—they couldn't go back to Paris or go any further south; they were trapped in a no-man's land with the Germans. Hannah sat in silence, thinking for a long while. When she looked up, the nun was gone.

She rose from the chair she didn't remember sitting down in, and went to go look for Eli. After checking outside first, she eventually found him in a small dining hall in the church, eating and messing about with another boy his age. She knew in that moment she would have to leave him.

She nodding at the nun, and then rummaged through her purse and pulled out his false papers. She handed them to Sister Mary Joan. The women exchanged looks, one pleading for his safety, the other promising it.

Hannah didn't intend to leave him there for long. She would find a job, a small but comfortable place not too far away, and she would be back to collect him soon. A month, she told herself, maybe two.

She waited until the meal was over and knelt down to say goodbye. The nun had advised her that it was best not to, that it would be easier on both of them if she slipped out unnoticed, but Hannah insisted.

Eli began to cry. Hannah tried to hide her own tears. Pulling Louise from the bag, she told Eli that as long as he had his bunny, it would be like she was there.

"Every night, you, me and Louise will meet in our dreams. Where should we meet? The park or the ice cream shop?"

Eli pondered for a moment, and then, excitedly, he exclaimed, "The zoo! We will meet at the zoo! Will Daddy be there too?"

"Of course." Hannah smiled. "We will all meet at the zoo. I will look for you there. And Louise will tell me if you are being a good boy. I love you."

"I love you mommy," Eli said.

After giving him one last hug, Hannah let the nun help her to her feet, walk her to the door and silently close it after her. Outside, Hannah finally let out the sob she had been holding in. She fought every maternal urge to beat at the door, grab Eli and take off running.

One foot at a time, she willed herself away from the door, then away from the steps, and then, finally, away from the church.

SYRIA

2014

T he day the letter came, Ahmed debated opening it immediately or waiting for Safia. What if this letter was like the one from Germany and the one from Australia? What if it too said that, while his credentials as a cardiac surgeon were impressive, they were not seeking to add to their current staff?

To be turned down for any position was disappointing, but these weren't simply jobs, they were visas for his family to leave Syria. This one was the last of the three he sent. St. James Hospital was a small, private, but well-regarded hospital that often catered to dignities, celebrities and the ultra-wealthy. It was also pioneering new medicine and cardiac procedures, and even though Ahmed would have accepted any of the positions, this was the one he really wanted. He couldn't handle another rejection letter no matter how politely it was phrased. He decided that if it was another no, it would be better to let Safia think that there had been no response at all. At least let her keep her hope.

He tore open the letter.

Dear Dr. Ahmed Bahar,
It is with supreme pleasure that we invite you to join our staff at St James hospital. We have reviewed your published articles and believe you will be a wonderful addition to our Cardiothoracic department. We would like you to start in the New Year, and will be in touch to help you make any arrangements to facilitate the move.

However, at this time we can only offer you a temporary work visa. After six months, we will be able to offer you a permanent work visa and visas for your family.

Please let us know at your earliest.

Thank you,
Dr. George Kaufman

Ahmed read the letter and reread it once more, silently wishing it had been a rejection letter. Safia would insist he go and he couldn't keep this from her. He folded the letter and placed it in his jacket pocket. The weight of decision made it feel heavier in his coat. And though it was only a piece of paper, he could feel it there for the rest of the day.

He should have been excited to show it to Safia, but he didn't when he arrived home, nor did he bring it up over super, nor when they were wrangling the children out of the bath and into their beds. He waited. And waited. Until finally, when they sat down to relax on the couch, he knew he could hold it in no more.

Their time on the couch was part of their nightly routine. It served two purposes: first, so they could spend some time with one another, discussing the day's events; second, the living room was directly beneath the children's bedrooms, so if any mischief was occurring, they would hear it. Once they were confident the children were asleep, they would either watch TV or sit quietly next to one another, each with a book. It quickly became Ahmed's favorite part of the day, though recently the discussions had become serious and hushed, now that the trouble that had been lurking in the background was inching closer and closer to them in Aleppo.

Ahmed had spent all day rehearsing how he'd bring it up and how he'd tell Safia that it would be a bad idea for him to leave the family. But he lost his nerve. He got up from the couch, went to his jacket and pulled the letter out. Handing it to her, he said nothing, but sat down cautiously on the coffee table directly in front of her.

A wave of concern passed Safia's face. She quickly scanned the letter and then let out a shriek of pure joy.

"I am so incredibly proud of you." She beamed, leaping up to hug and kiss him.

"But did you see about the visas?"

"Six months is nothing! I can handle the children and the household. In fact, this may be even better, as you can go ahead and get things established. We can't very well move a family of five into a hotel."

"I think it unwise to you leave you here alone."

"You are going, that's all there is to it. We will tell the children at breakfast."

"But—"

"It is settled, Ahmed. This is what is best for our family and you! I will not debate it any further," she said, grinning.

Ahmed felt both elated and guilty. He knew this would be the outcome, but it felt selfish. Safia too felt conflicted. She knew that it was indeed troubling times and she didn't want him to go, but as she had told him, it was best for the family. And beyond the family, it was a professional opportunity of a lifetime. She wouldn't keep him from it. It was the best option of bad options.

At breakfast, the children looked puzzled more than anything.

"Where is London?" Nadir asked.

Ahmed quickly went to the small library in his office,

pulled an old atlas from the shelf and brought it back to the kitchen, where he placed it on the table and opened it up to the first page. "We are here," he said, pointing, "and there is London."

This new revelation inspired only more confusion amongst the children.

Over the coming days, more and more questions would come from the twins:

"What about my friends?"

"What about my toys?"

"Why can't we come now?"

"Will there be snow?"

"How long will you be gone?"

Soon the questions ceased and the reality of Ahmed leaving began to set in. There was never a good moment to leave your family, but this felt particularly bad. Thousands of people were leaving the city daily, many of them leaving family behind, and now he was one of them.

It was safer for Ahmed to travel alone to Damascus, so on the morning of his flight, he said his farewells in the foyer of his house.

"Nadir, you are the man of the house now. Look after your sister, mother and baby brother," he said as he gave him a tight hug.

"Asma, be obedient to your mother and be kind to your brothers." The little girl nodded sadly. The night before she had thrown herself on the floor wailing for him not to go, not without her. The commotion had elicited the same response from Nadir, and in an attempt to garner some sleep, he had let all five of them climb into their bed.

He kissed Asma in the head, and then gave another kiss to Salim who was asleep in Safia's arms.

Turning to Safia, he said, "I am only a flight away." It was meant to sound reassuring but came out with the tone of an apology.

She nodded, wiping tears from the corners of her eyes. "We will see you very soon."

She hugged him with one arm, trying not to crush Salim between them.

He gave her one last kiss, looked at his family, and smiled. He then picked up his suitcase and left, before they could see him start to cry.

Had Ahmed known what would come in the following months, he would have never left.

But the sun was shining, and after he started his new job, six months would go quickly enough, he reassured himself.

BACK TO PARIS

1945

H annah was determined to make it to Paris, even if it meant she had to walk there. David would be there; she could feel it. She borrowed enough money for train fare and went as far as she could, but the lines were jammed with people coming and going. Still, she had come this far, and now she was only day away from the city by foot.

She walked and walked, but she was too hot and tired from the journey and the August heat. She found a large tree by the side of the road and sat down to rest under its shade, folding her jacket as a makeshift pillow. She laid on her back against the cool earth and must have drifted asleep, because the next thing she knew, she was startled awake by a car horn honking.

Looking around to see where the sound had come from, she saw a Jeep with a young American behind the wheel. She felt weary, even more so because in the sun, this golden haired boy looked like he had stepped right off a Hollywood movie set. She smoothed her hair and dress and walked over to see why he was honking.

"Are you alright, ma'am?" he said slowly.

Hannah looked at him blankly. She didn't speak English.

The man tried again, even slower, sounding out each syllable, but still to no avail. His thick southern drawl did not help matters.

Hannah pointed. "Paris."

"Hop in," he said cheerfully.

Hannah didn't move, so the man walked around the Jeep, opened the door and gestured for her to get in, which she did. The man put the Jeep into gear and off they went. She closed her eyes as the breeze hit her face. It was still hot, but it was a welcome reprieve from the stifling air.

"Theo," the man said, as he patted his chest.

"Hannah," she said in reply, replicating the gesture, then extended her hand. For the first time, she was conscious of how dirty she was.

Hannah held on for dear life as they hurtled down the roads. The man drove the Jeep like he was being chased by Satan himself, always honking and swerving violently. Theo seemed to be having great fun, and he laughed at Hannah's slightly terrified expression. She began a conversation, only for the purpose of getting him to slow down, as the wind made it hard to hear. The language barrier didn't stop either of them from talking, though their conversation moved at a very pace, in fragmented sentences. Theo explained he was from some place called "Montgomery."

Theo offered her water, which she declined, and a cigarette, which, to Theo's surprise, she accepted.

When he dropped her off on the edge of the city, Hannah thanked him repeatedly. If she had had money, she would have offered him some, but she knew it didn't matter. He wouldn't have accepted it anyway.

The ride and the refreshing spirit of the young man had been good for her, and Hannah allowed herself to hope that when she reached their apartment, David would be waiting for them. Once in the city, it was as if she could feel a gravitational pull to their building. She picked up her pace the closer she got. And then she was actually there.

Unsure what she was going to find, she steadied her nerves, but still allowed herself to become overwhelmed with a sense of hope. Should she knock? It was her home, after all. There was a spare key hidden in the courtyard, which she retrieved and moved toward the building.

"Please let him be there," she said aloud but to no one.

Climbing the stairs, her heart raced. And then,

suddenly, a woman appeared at the door to the apartment, Hannah's apartment. What if David had thought they were dead? Could it be possible? But then three children emerged behind her. The woman stopped dead when she saw Hannah.

"Who are you?!" Hannah demanded, perhaps louder than she intended.

"Lisette Moreau," the woman responded, confused.

"What are you doing in my apartment?" She was shouting now.

"You must be mistaken. This is our apartment," Lisette said, pushing the smallest child behind her, sensing that Hannah was becoming unhinged.

The spectacle had drawn onlookers from the other apartments in the building, none of whom Hannah recognized. Finally, she saw Madame Boyer, the perpetually crabby old woman who always complained about Bernard and Eli playing in the courtyard. She was always complaining about something. There was especially no love lost for the Jewish tenants.

Hannah turned to woman, silently pleading for an explanation.

"Go away, there is nothing for you here," Madame Boyer snapped.

"What?"

"You heard me. Get out of here. If you knew what was

good for you, you would have died with your husband and the rest of them."

The commotion had lured more neighbors from their apartments, and even more curious bystanders from the street, who stood on the edge of the courtyard looking on, waiting to see what would happen next. No one watching came to Hannah's defense, each of them telling themselves that these women must know each other so it must be a personal fight. Yet, they still hovered.

The screaming escalated, with Madame Boyer directing her anger at Hannah. "I know the truth about you! If he is dead it's because of you."

At that, Hannah slapped the woman so hard that Madame Boyer landed flat on her back. "Get up, and I'll kill you," she said in sharp tone.

Madame Boyer stayed on the ground.

"THATS RIGHT!!" she yelled, when, out of the corner of her eye, she realized just how many people were watching. "STAND THERE AND WATCH."

Madame Boyer, determined to get the last word, pointed at Hannah and screamed, "Collaborator!"

Hannah turned on her heels, throwing the spare key, which had still been in her hand, at Madame Boyer. She grabbed her suitcase and, still fueled by hatred, left as fast as she could. Once away, she sat down on curb and cried.

She felt someone touch her shoulder. It was an elderly gentlemen, and he was offering her a handkerchief. He explained that he had moved into the building a couple of years ago, and while he did not know about any former residents, he would keep an eye out for a man showing up looking for her. He took a small pad from his pocket and wrote down Hannah's name. He promised that if he found her husband, he would pass along news that she, in turn, was looking for him.

Hannah spent countless days in Paris trying to find David. One record office directed her to the next, the Red Cross told her to try the Jewish Refugee Committee, who told her to go back to the Red Cross. Lists of survivors were being compiled, but no one yet had a complete list.

The information she was able to gather painted a hopeless picture. David had been rounded up mere days after she and Eli left. From there, like all the others, he was transported to Drancy. After that, she didn't know. He would have been sent East, no matter his fate, so eastward she would go. If he was alive, he would most likely be in a displaced person's camp. But it was possible—she was told, as David was young and fit—that he had been sent to a camp for work detail.

She was one in a sea of between seven and eleven million refugees, all moving around attempting to find one another.

But first, she had somewhere else to go. She must head back south, and pray with every ounce of faith she had left that Eli had remained safe.

LONDON

2015

L ondon greeted Ahmed the way it greeted most, with a cold March rain. The weather made Ahmed feel more isolated than ever before. He questioned himself the entire flight: was he doing the right thing? The first thing he did was grab postcards, albeit those depicting a sunnier England, for the kids, one for each, even for Salim. Of course, he wouldn't know if they'd read them, let alone received them, but the thought was there all the same. He called Safia to tell her that he had arrived safely, but as he had taken the latest flight possible, it was late, and her voice was filled with sleep. Whispering to mimic her voice, he told her he would call back tomorrow.

He had found a room to rent in Hackney from a man who claimed to be musician. What instrument he played seemed to be undecided. The man's mother was also living there and had an obsession with cooking beets. It was clean enough, and had all the necessities. Ahmed could have afforded a lovely home but thought it best to save his money until his family arrived. After all, he reasoned, he would be working most of the time, so would only really need a place to sleep.

Arriving at the hospital, Ahmed was struck by how much it didn't look like a hospital at all. It was not cold nor clinical, but warm and inviting. He was given the tour and introduced to more people his brain would allow space for names. Nothing seemed too foreign, or new. Medicine was a universal language and St. James hospital was pioneering techniques never used before. Ahmed assured himself that six months would pass by quickly.

Night after night, it was his long conversations with Safia that drove him, and the anticipation of hearing her voice each night made it hard for him to focus on work. He was so distracted by the news out of Syrian and homesick for his family, all he wanted was to go home. But Safia assured him that, despite the news, their family was safe and that he should stay for the time being.

By July, word came of a mass exodus from Aleppo. Food was becoming scarce and medical access even more limited. Safia had told him that she had become a midwife of sorts. As medical attention was being directed to the injured, there were no beds left for expectant mothers. She had delivered twelve babies before August, and with the city under partial siege, it was far easier for her to travel to them, than them attempting to get to the hospital only to be turned away. In one particular conversation about this, Safia had broken down sobbing, as she told Ahmed about a stillbirth, one that she was certain would have been a healthy baby with proper medical intervention.

The next morning Ahmed went to see Dr. Kaufman, and explained the dire situation and his need for immediate visas. Dr. Kaufman looked at him, slightly puzzled.

"You, of course, have met Dr. Stevens?" he asked.

"Of course, I have."

Ahmed had not given it any thought that there were two doctors with the same specialty on staff at this relatively small hospital. In that moment, it became clear that the six months were not a waiting period, as he had guessed, but a trial period in which he was competing against Dr. Stevens.

"My family is a danger," Ahmed stated, not feeling the need to explain any further.

"I am sorry, my hands are tied until the position is filled on a permanent basis."

"Then I am leaving to join them."

"Do what you must, but if you leave I will be forced to give the position to Dr. Stevens."

Ahmed stared at him in disbelief. This man could not

be serious. How could he be so heartless? His eyes burned into Dr. Kaufman's.

"I am not an uncaring man. I know you are worried for you children…"

Ahmed had turned and walked out at that, closing the door behind him, not wanting to hear Dr. Kaufman's attempts to clear his own guilt with anecdotes and analogies. Ahmed had been lied to, or at least led to believe something that was not true.

Immediately, he called Safia. He guessed she had her hands full, if the background noise of the children laughing and screaming to one another was anything to go by. He was mentally preparing himself to tell her what Dr. Kaufman had said when he heard a loud crash.

"Asma!" Safia screamed angrily before telling Ahmed that she would have to call him back. She'd hung up before he even had a moment to get another word in.

He sat with his head in his hands. He hadn't yet changed into his scrubs for the day, and an old woman patted him on the back, thinking he must be distraught over a patient.

"There, there, I am sure they will be fine," she said with a smile.

Ahmed waited patiently for Safia to call him back, but an hour turned into two, then five, then twenty-four. He left her a voicemail every half hour or so till her voicemail was full, but still no call. What if the crash he had heard was something worse? Were they safe?

By time Safia phoned him back, his stomach was aching and his head pounded. She told him what the morning news had confirmed: ground fighting had begun in Aleppo.

He would not be returning to his family anytime soon. Him being in London was the plan, the only plan to get his family out safely. Ahmed didn't tell Safia about the visas, or Dr. Stevens. She sounded so hopeful, saying they only had to endure a few more months and then their nightmare would be over. Ahmed couldn't be there to comfort her or ease his children's fears, so he wouldn't take away the one thing he had left to give, hope.

GERMANY

1946-1947

When Hannah returned to collect Eli after the war had ended she was shell of her former self. Her glossy brown hair had greyed and the light behind her green eyes had faded. How—or where—she had survived the war, Eli didn't know, only that the last four years had not been kind to her. He tried to ask about it, more than once, but all she would say was, "it doesn't matter; it is in the past."

That day when he saw her standing in the church waiting for him, Eli was convinced he was looking at a ghost. When she called out "Eli!" he had frozen in his tracks. He remembered that that was his name, but no one had called him that in years. It was a strange reunion. While they were both happy to be reunited, there was little joy in that moment. Eli packed a few things, a sweater that was far too large, some bread and cheese the nuns had given him and, of course, his bunny, Louise.

Eli would always look back fondly on the time he spent in the orphanage. As an adult, he tried to recall if there had ever been any danger. Had Nazi's ever come? But for the life of him, he could not remember. What he did remember was the fun and games, the picnics and mischief with the older boys. Were those innocent games of hide-go-seek more sinister than he remembered? Were there more to those times he remembered hiding in a cupboard in the kitchen? Had his young mind shielded him from the danger? Eli remembered being angry when his mother declared they were leaving. He didn't want to leave. In future years he would question if, indeed, he would have been better off growing up as Alexander.

It was once they were on their way that Hannah informed Eli that they were not returning to Paris, but to a place called Stuttgart in Germany. That is where they would stay until they could be reunited with his father.

"Germany?" he asked, puzzled. He had been shielded from the war but even he knew that that was the enemy.

"Yes, we are leaving France like I told you."

"But aren't the Germans the bad guys?" he had asked. Ever since leaving the orphanage, almost nothing had made any sense to him.

"At least they are honest about it," his mother said.

Eli would always hate Germany, not for broad, ideological reasons, but because of the awfulness he saw there. His mother may have had nowhere else to go or may have been searching for his father, but bringing him into Germany directly after the war exposed him to everything he had been shielded from. His mother also believed that by being in an American zone, it would help get them to America.

Being only nine, Eli didn't quite understand how they came to be at the DP camp. Looking back, all he remembered was the lice, the cold and the meager rations. He remembered very few other children, and the children who were there were sickly thin. There was no one to play with, Eli's only joy was following the American's around, asking for chocolate or to put on their helmets.

Much of that time lived in fragmented memories. Even as an adult, he couldn't be sure whether he actually didn't recall those details or whether his mind had merely blocked it out.

Cold and hungry would become his new normal, with damp clothes that were always dank. His mother was there of course, but with the news that his father had been sent first to Drancy and then to Auschwitz, she retreated into herself. She still breathed, but ceased to be among the living. She didn't intend to neglect Eli, but she was barely capable of keeping herself alive. She became perpetually sick with a cough that would not cease.

Auschwitz. The word hung in the air. Everyone around Eli seemed to know what that meant. He couldn't grasp where this place, *Auschwitz*, was, or why they couldn't go there to find his dad. Finally, his mother explained it to him, the best anyone could explain to a nine year old. Eli failed to comprehend, and for years, he would hold out hope that there had been some sort of mistake, and like them, his dad was in a different DP camp looking for them.

"We have to go home!" Eli shouted at his mother one day, his voice piercing the cold silence.

"France is not our home anymore! It never was!"

"But he will come looking for us. He won't be able to find us here!" Eli stated, becoming visibly shaken. "We have to go back to Paris!"

"I went to Paris, Eli. There are strangers living in our house. Strangers who watched your father be dragged from that place. Don't you understand? He is not coming Eli."

"You don't know that, you can't be sure!" Eli screamed even louder, and then ran out of the tiny room they shared. Hannah tried to catch him but her lungs burned and she nearly collapsed in a coughing fit.

They couldn't stay in the camp forever, but Hannah would not even consider returning to France. They were indeed like everyone else there: stuck, unable to return home and with no means to create a new one. American visas, though easier to obtain now than when the war began, were still nearly impossible to come by, especially as they had no family stateside.

Without visas to America, British Mandate Palestine became the only option. Hannah watched people leave every day, albeit illegally. Illegal crossings were not something Hannah had any intention of attempting again, but when in March, with permission of the Americans, 200 German police officers raided the DP camp under the guise of looking for stolen items, she had to reevaluate. Many of those who had been liberated from concentration camps were woken again to the horror of the Germans. Chaos ensued, leaving one DP dead, others injured, and the rest severely traumatized. She realized that not even the Americans would protect her and Eli.

Now that she knew that David would never come, Hannah vowed that she would take Eli away from the horridness that was Europe. And so she arranged passage for her and Eli to Israel.

ALEPPO ATTACK

2015

With Ahmed gone, Safia tried to keep things as normal as possible for the children, but she could feel the noose of Aleppo tightening around their necks. She kept telling herself that they had already lived through the worst of it. But as the violence ramped up in the city, Safia no longer felt comfortable hiding out in her own home waiting for their visas to come through.

She began volunteering at night at the hospital. Babies were still being born and, while she still delivered her fair share, most days she was treating gunshot wounds or burns from motor shells. It wasn't her specialty, but any doctor was a better than no doctor. It was a warzone. Safia often found herself at a maternity home that had been set up on the border between eastern and western. Doctors were fleeing the city and there were not enough as it was; no one could attend to those bringing life into this world, so Safia did what she could.

Still, it would be only a few months more until they could leave. Ahmed often floated the idea of returning, but she scolded him for such an idea. They needed visas and if he returned, they would be stuck.

The main hospital was walking distance from the house. Ahmed and Safia had chosen it for this very reason, that they'd need it for when they decided to try for a large family. Safia would leave Asma and Nadir with their elderly neighbor, Faiza, who didn't mind watching over two sleeping children, And Salim would come with Safia—he was a little much for Faiza to handle. She would drop him off at the nursery where he would happily coo and flirt with the nurses. Safia would check in periodically, often teasing the nurses that it would be okay if he didn't sleep in someone's arms, insisting that they were spoiling him.

Safia hated to admit it, but she had become almost used to the violence around her. And then on March 16, everything changed again. She hadn't planned to work on that particular night, but her phone rang and on the other side of the phone a nurse frantically told her she had to come. She couldn't explain why, only that something had happened. Safia handed all three children to Faiza, apologizing profusely, and ran to the hospital.

The sight that greeted her was one of immense horror.

The hallways were filled with people choking. There was chaos every which way she looked. The hallways were lined with people, and she saw a man seizing on the floor. She was able to grab a doctor. Her eyes asked the question her mouth couldn't form.

"There has been a chemical attack. We think chlorine or a nerve gas," the doctor said as he kept moving. There had been rumors of chemical attacks but they had only been that—rumors, the same as the kidnappings and disappearances. Everyone had heard of it but there was never anyone who'd actually been there. Safia only stopped for the briefest of moments to ponder which side had deployed such an awful tool.

She jumped in to help wherever she could, but triage was a mess of people. She did her best, but it was clear that some of those waiting were already on the brink of death, and some had even already passed away. She shouted to those waiting to remove their clothes, as they were soaked in chemicals, and she pushed every dose of atropine the hospital had on supply—the doctors were unsure what chemical was used in the attack so it was the only thing they could think to do. The smell of chlorine was so strong the doctors ordered every single window opened, but it was too late: nurses and doctors alike began to show symptoms simply from being in proximity to those they were treating. Safia had to dose herself with the only antidote they had. Still, from that one attack, an official estimated that 200 people had died, a number that Safia considered too low to be true.

She worked for two days straight before returning home and collapsing. When she awoke, she called Ahmed in tears. There were no words, so Ahmed just listened to her sob. She was scared and she wanted out of Syria. It was one thing for fights between rebels and the army, but the memory of those children gasping for breath was more than she could bear. Ahmed sobbed when he hung up. He couldn't see a way to get his family's visas as urgently as he needed them, and ff he returned home for too long, his own visa would be revoked. More than that, if he left and missed any surgeries, the position would go to Dr. Stevens. While the stakes were very different, both men wanted the prestigious position.

While Ahmed competed, Safia waited .They were both in limbo.

Safia took a week off before returning to the hospital. Even though it had been deep cleaned, she could still smell the chlorine and stench of death in the air. She did the best she could to be present for her patients, but the only way she was coping was by allowing her mind to drift to the new life she would have in London. She pictured long walks through green parks and the kids running about. Her conversations with Ahmed on their daily phone calls became filled with housing plans, ideas of where to educate the children and a list of restaurants Ahmed wanted to take Safia to. Ahmed had only been renting a renting room, but he promised her the home of her dreams when she arrived. It would only be a few more months, and so, looking only forward to her future life helped get her through each day.

May 27th began like any other day, with Safia doing her best to keep the children entertained before she headed to work. Salim was exceptionally fussy as he had begun to grow in his molars. Safia debated calling into work but carried a grumpy Salim on her hip to the hospital.

What happened that night, or who she treated, she couldn't recall, as her memories were dominated by the bomb. She only remembered the lights flickering and the floor dropping out from underneath her. She heard explosions and saw the building across the street disappearing under dust and fire. Her heart dropped as she realized that that building was a school. Many doctors ran out to try to find the wounded. Safia did not, as she ran up the stairs instead, to the nursery where Salim was.

Those doctors who had ran to help were then hit by another bomb that took out the emergency room entrance. The upper floors of the hospital were then destroyed by yet another, including the nursery. Such an attack seemed beyond the rules of war, but hospitals all over the city had been targeted. At least ten medical facilities, including a maternity home were hit with aerial bombardment. Doctors brave enough to stay were found guilty of treating the rebels, and lived in fear. Safia herself had never stopped to ask whose child she was delivering or who had been gassed—so she too could have been guilty of aiding the enemy.

Safia felt warm blood on her face. Someone was shouting in her direction, but she couldn't hear them. The stairwell had crumbled around her but except for a nasty head wound and busted eardrums, she was among the lucky. But she stood there, staring up at the sky; the sky was where the nursery had been, where Salim had been. It was then the darkness enveloped her.

***

Ahmed was on the first flight to Damascus. He'd tried Safia's phone and the home line repeatedly, but he couldn't get through. He called every last person he could think of. Most promised to keep an ear out, but they knew nothing more than that the hospital had been bombed. Desperation led him to the airport and onto a flight. He would go to his family and cradle them in his arms. He would not let his mind entertain any other possibility.

Safia barely noticed the pain in her head. Her colleagues had diagnosed a concussion and given her seventeen stitches to her forehead. They urged her to stay, but she had to get to Asma and Nadir. She made her way out of the hospital, disoriented but determined. The sunlight momentarily blinded her in a way that she felt lost, but she then realized it was because the building, the landmarks she had always unconsciously used to orient herself were gone, now shadows of their former selves. She ran toward home, and for the first time, felt the splitting pain in her head. With each heavy step she took, it felt as if someone was hitting her again on the back of her head. When the pain became so intense, she slowed only for a minute, thinking that she might black out.

She rounded the corner and saw had once been her home, the entire front gone like a child's doll house. She could see into her dining room, and saw the children's bikes still by the foot of the door. She climbed over the rubble, falling and clawing her way toward the threshold. She could see then what she couldn't see from the street: part of the floor had collapsed and the entire back of the house was now a heap of rubble. She let out a wail, and then another. Time stood still as she sat on her knees, screaming for Asma, Nadir and Salim. She heard the sound of the wailing but did not register that it was coming from her own mouth.

She felt hands on her shoulders, shaking her back to reality. Someone was shouting at her but she couldn't understand. Snapping back into the moment, Safia recognized that it was Ali, Faiza's husband.

"They are safe! They are safe!" he kept repeating over and over again.

She grabbed on to him, hugging him tightly, and he led her away from the rubble to his house. As soon as they approached, Asma and Nadir ran to her. As she held them close, Safia promised herself she would never let go of them ever again.

Faiza pressed a warm cup of tea into her hands, and began to explain. "I had made Kanafeh that afternoon, and promised some to the children before bed if they were good. I knew you wouldn't mind. I left a note on your kitchen table so you'd know where we were, should you return early. But then the bombing started. We heard the hospital took a direct hit, and we assumed the worst. Ali went to try to find out about you and Salim." She only whispered Salim's name, knowing better than to ask any questions. "But it was chaos. And so we kept the children and kept hoping and praying. Ali kept watch on your house, knowing that you, if you were able to, would return there. It is a miracle you survived."

Faiza let her use her phone, and Safia tried to call Ahmed, but he didn't answer. She didn't know what to do. This didn't happen to people like her. She was going to take her children and leave this place of horror. But where would she go? Her thoughts rolled through her head faster than she could process them. Damascus was technically closer, but what kind of things would she have to go through to get there? She couldn't put her and the children on a plane without passports. She could cross into Turkey but what would she do once there? And where was Ahmed? He was coming, she could feel it. She would wait for him. Faiza and Ali would never turn her out.

But another problem presented itself: Nadir's medicine. He had always been a sickly child, and not long before his fifth birthday, Safia and Ahmed were able to confirm what they suspected: juvenile diabetes. His condition was easily managed and rarely cause for second thought in normal times, but along with the house being destroyed, so was the supply of insulin. The vial Faiza had brought from Safia's house for what was meant to be quick visit was dangerously low. The hospital supply was also depleting, with vials disappearing in the night and sold on the black market for 600% times the price.

Safia debated with herself for only a brief moment. As a doctor she should know better, but she returned to the hospital and stole two vials. That would be enough to keep him safe once they left Aleppo. She knew Dr. Tahan witnessed her in the act, but Safia said nothing and rushed out. If Ahmed was coming she couldn't wait.

"Safia!" Dr. Tahan called out after her.

She quickened her steps. Dr. Tahan had studied with her and Ahmed in medical school, and she considered him to be one of their oldest friends, but even for him, she would not hand back what she had stolen.

"Wait, please," Dr. Tahan called out.

Safia turned to face him with a sad but stubborn look in her eyes.

"I saw you take the insulin. I don't care. I know what happened to Salim," he said, and then continued. "My wife and her brother's family are leaving the city, headed to Turkey. Their father was killed in the strike. They are leaving tonight. There is no reason for anyone to stay. There is room for you and the children, if you want. It might be easier to get London via Ankara. I hear conditions are bad in the camps, but…" He made a sweeping gesture to the destruction around them, and gave a small chuckle.

Knowing that others were making the journey, Safia decided that she would not stay in Aleppo any longer. She thanked Dr. Tahan profusely and rushed home to gather the children. She tried once again to reach Ahmed, but the lines wouldn't connect. She was able to leave word at St. James hospital that she and the children were going to Turkey. She thought for a moment of trying to collect some things from the house, but when she saw what was left of her ruined home again, she realized that there was nothing in there she would risk her life for. Her two oldest children were safe and that was all that mattered. She would have to flee with only the clothes on their backs, like so many others had.

Safia tried once more to call Ahmed, before leaving Aleppo once and for all. Deep down, she knew why he wasn't answering: he was trying to make his way to her. All the same, she left a voice message warning him. She couldn't bring herself to say everything she needed to say, so she only said, "Ahmed, there is nothing left for us in Aleppo. Please do not come, we won't be there. I am taking Nadir and Asma to Turkey with relatives of Dr. Tahan. I will call again soon, my love."

Ahmed heard the voicemail as he arrived at the Damascus airport, and even though she had not said it, Ahmed knew that Salim was gone. He sat down in the terminal and wept. The business of the airport continued around him but, for Ahmed, time stopped.

GERMANY TO PARIS TO MARSEILLES

1946

After the raid, the fear that consumed Hannah seemed to reanimate her. She quickly set upon a path, first to get out of Germany, and then to get out of Europe. When Eli had heard that they were headed to Paris, he had breathed a sigh of relief, knowing that finally they were going home. His mother must have been mistaken, and his dad would be there. He was more than pleased when they were back in France. But Hannah shared none of this excitement. For her, it was a means to an end. Eli remembered walking for days on end, his feet blistered and bleeding. But still, Hannah pushed them forward to Paris, moving as if she were possessed.

In Paris, Hannah went to a man for two rail tickets to Marseille. Eli felt as if it was the first time he had seen a living person since the convent, and he deemed the man sinister as he spoke in only hushed tones as he wished them well on their journey. He also arranged for them to stay the night with a lovely French woman named Sabine. She was a rather large woman who had a contagious laugh. She gave Eli a small container of sweets before sending him out to play with the neighborhood children. This made Eli immediately this most popular child in the arron-dissement. The deprivation from the war was still a very real thing, and for the kids, the candy was more than a simple luxury. For a moment, it felt as if there had been no war, and all was right in the world. When he came back in, covered in dirt, Sabine kissed both of his cheeks, evidently delighted by what anyone else would have seen as a naughty child. Eli played in a bath Sabine ran for him until it went cold, and then climbed into the fresh clothes she had laid out for him. Eli didn't know where the clothes had come from, but when Sabine exclaimed how handsome he looked, he blushed.

Still, Eli didn't understand why they couldn't return home. They had to be close. Eli resolved that he would make his way home the following day, with or without his mother, but by the light of the next morning, Eli and Hannah were on a train to Marseille. Eli tried to protest, but Hannah shot him a look that told him *that* conversation would not be taking place again.

Eli watched the fields whiz by. He grew antsy on the trip. Sabine had packed them a few small sandwiches, which they devoured as the day slipped away. She had also handed Hannah a few francs—nothing much, but it was so much more about the gesture than the money itself.

"Celeste?" a middle-aged man in three-piece suit asked, looking at Hannah.

"I am sorry, you must be mistaken," she said, staring straight ahead.

"It's me, Jean. We met at that party at the Ritz last year. That was some night, right?!" He chuckled.

"My name is Hannah, and this is my son Eli," she said, gesturing toward Eli.

"Huh, I guess I am mistaken." He leaned over and whispered something to her, and then added, "Remember—Hôtel Louvre et Paix if you change your mind."

Hannah said nothing more and the man disappeared. Eli asked what he had said, but all that his mother would say was that the man was mistaken and was looking for someone else.

It was a beautiful day in Marseille. The journey from Germany to Paris had been chilly and muddy, but the sun shone bright and the sky was clear. Either way, Eli was relieved to be off the train. Between the two of them, everything Eli and Hannah owned fit in one small suitcase. This made it easier for Hannah to once again find her fixed determination as she hurried them away from the train station. She kept looking back, and only stopped when she was several streets away. Only then did she ask for directions to the address on the paper the sinister man had given her. In her haste, she had taken them in the wrong direction, so they had to detour back around the train station before arriving at the home of yet another stranger. Eli hoped that there would be kids to play with, but he wasn't so lucky this time. While the owners were friendly, they were old, and the house had a quietness that was uncomfortable. There were all sorts of curious trinkets on the shelves. Eli wondered what they were for and the urge to touch them was almost more than he could bear, but he knew that he shouldn't touch anything. His mother, sensing his willpower would not last much longer, took him for a walk.

This was the first time Eli saw the sea, and he was surprised by the sheer size of it. He had always known it was there, but seeing it was an entirely different thing. His mother explained that in two days they would board one of the large ships and set sail for Palestine. He had heard of this place when they were in Stuttgart, but from what he had heard, it sounded like a place you couldn't get to.

Hannah stared out at the sea. The sun reflecting off it stung her eyes, but she could only look forward and not turn back. They were about to leave France, forever.

FLIGHT TO TURKEY

2015

Making it to the border of Turkey was easier than anyone had anticipated. No one said a word in the van, even the ever-excitable Asma. There had been chaos in Aleppo: people screaming, distant gunshots and the beginning of what would be one of the largest mass exoduses in modern history. They had no directions, but they followed the flow of humans.

Safia stared out the window, lost in her thoughts. She thought about those on the road they had passed, some carrying every belonging they could, others clearly injured; she thought about Salim; but more than anything, she thought about Ahmed. With or without the voicemail, by now he would know. Would he blame her? Would he blame himself? What would they do now? The sight of the massive amount of people ahead snapped her back into the moment.

There was a sea of humanity waiting at the border. Safia knew people had been fleeing since the start of the war but it had never occurred to her that she would be among them. Turkey had been a beacon of hope for so many, but now the influx seemed too great for any one country to absorb. They had built a 500-mile fence to prevent people from crossing, so everyone huddled into checkpoints. Yusef, who was barely seventeen, was shaking. Laia, Dr. Tahan's wife, told him it was to be expected. She was younger than Safia expected, maybe all of twenty years old, but despite her youth, Laia was exceptionally kind and calm, offering both children plums when they became agitated. To Safia, she seemed sweet but naïve.

A Turkish guard who was making his way around stopped to ask some questions. Laia and her brother explained that they already had family in the camp that lay just beyond the border. You could make out the lights in the distance, but the place felt a world away. The officer then turned his sights on Safia, Asma and Nadir. He was particularly curious about Laia's and Safia's husbands, and he was not so subtle in his questions. Safia angrily explained that both were married women and, like everyone else, were fleeing because Aleppo had become too dangerous. She started to tell of the gassing and then the bombing; she explained as much as she could but choked up as she got to the part of the story about Salim. The officer's face softened, and he shook his head.

"This is a nice van," he said to Yusef.

Yusef nodded, but didn't say anything, Laia leaned over, grinning. "Yes, it is a shame we will have to leave it here and cross on foot. If the border ever opens, of course." Laia wasn't as simple as she had seemed.

"Well, we are not allowing vehicles to cross at this time, but..." He let his gaze wander, as if he wasn't sure what he would say next, but Laia had known to expect this. Her aunt and uncle had made the crossing the previous winter, and like now, the border had been closed. But it had magically opened for her Aunt's emerald ring.

She played along, giving a coquettish smile. "It would be such a shame to leave it here, but if we cannot cross, we should turn around before we run out of Petrol. Let's go, Yusef" Yusef looked at his sister, confused, but she nodded and he began to turn the engine over.

"Wait!" the guard interjected, revealing his hand.

Laia smiled, knowing that the ruse had worked.

They were allowed to enter Turkey, and the officer had won himself a new minivan. Yusef seemed bothered by the whole transaction, but in Laia's mind, the van had served its purpose. She winked at Safia.

The camp, Kilis, was nothing like Safia had expected. It was clean, with a wide street down the middle. Homes were small but tidy, built out of containers. They walked past a school, a mosque and a hospital. There was not a tent to be seen, or anything like the horrors she had imagined that so often accompany the word "camp." She let out a deep breath she hadn't been aware she was holding in.

After asking a few passersby for help, they were able to locate the home of Laia's aunt and uncle. It was a small, prefabricated container, but it had three rooms, including a kitchen sink and a small bathroom. It was by no one's standards luxurious, but it was clean and functional. Laia's aunt, Ajda, busied herself making sure they were fed, while her uncle, Muhammed, sat in the corner reading a paper. Occasionally, he would look over the corner of the paper and nod, but he was not talkative. As Safia, Aida and Laia took over the cooking and rotating the children in and out the shower, Yusef instinctively joined Muhammed.

"You and your children are most welcome to stay here tonight and for the next couple of nights," Ajda said as they made preparations for dinner. "Laia told me what happened. I am so sorry for your loss. There are too many stories like this."

Safia nodded, not knowing what to say.

"Tomorrow, I will help you and Laia and Yusef get

registered. The refugee council will help with food and housing, school for the children and to help you get settled here."

"I don't plan on being here long."

"No one ever does."

THE MORESBY

1947

A much more famous ship would soon leave this port, with the same destination. It was called the Exodus 1947, and some would claim it was the ship that would launch the nation of Israel. Its fate and outcome were unknown to Hannah and Eli and the 800 others on that March day when they boarded The Moresby. The boarding was chaotic, but Eli loved watching the sailors shout orders back and forth, or toss cargo from the shore. For a little boy, he felt like a great explorer.

The ship was old but seaworthy, Eli had heard someone say. It was not as Eli had thought it would be; he had pictured a ship with fancy dining rooms and comfortable beds. But here, there was a meager dining hall with long benches bolted to the floor, and a deck below, almost too tight to navigate, with rows upon rows of bunk beds. But, as Eli was watching people embark, his spirits lifted when he saw other children. He desperately missed the children from the convent, and he suspected that he would not see them again.

As the boat pushed off from the dock, Eli insisted that they go up to wave goodbye. Hannah insisted that there would be no one to wave to, but she eventually relented. She couldn't help but smile as Eli waved vigorously to the dock workers, who indulged him by waving back. Eli wasn't the only child who had had this idea; there were half a dozen other children doing the same.

"Children are so resilient," Hannah heard someone nearby say. Her French was not that of a native speaker, and Hannah turned to see a young woman. She introduced herself as Vera.

"Which one is yours?" Vera asked.

Hannah gestured toward Eli, who was still waving as the shore receded from view.

"And you?" Hannah asked, though the youngest child Hannah could see was maybe six or seven and the woman looked to only be in her early twenties.

Vera smiled. "None of them—but technically I am in charge of those seven right there." Hannah looked at her, perplexed. "Orphans," the young woman added. Hannah's stomach dropped for a moment. She wondered how far she would have to go to stop seeing so many reminders of a world that had been shattered.

It didn't take long for conditions on the ship to deteriorate. The stench was overpowering. Many on board had been ill before they had boarded, and sea-sickness took hold of many others. Hannah and Eli found their escape on deck most days. The breeze was cold, but the sun felt nice on their skin. She often saw Vera doing the same with her gaggle of children.

The two women would strike up friendly conversation as the children played games neither of them could comprehend. Vera stumbled over her French, so the conversation was mixture of broken French and German. Hannah learned that Vera was Viennese-born and that she immigrated to Palestine against her family's wishes. Now, she was a volunteer for The "Bricha". Immigration was still illegal but this did not stop those like Vera from volunteering to bring as many refugees as they could. This was her third trip, and including the seven on board, she had accompanied thirty-eight orphaned children over the border.

"Did the ships make it?" Hannah asked. Rumors were rife aboard the ship, as people had nothing to do but wait, spread gossip and hope. Another rumor was that the ship, if caught, would be sent back to Europe; others said that they were setting up prison camps in Palestine. The worst rumor of all was that those attempting to enter were being shot. Hannah convinced herself that that couldn't possibly be true, but her mind flashed back to the last time she had tried to cross, the image of the woman and her small daughter lying in the mud.

"The smaller of the ships was able to get past the blockade and dock in Caesarea. The other was intercepted by a destroyer," Vera said as she stared straight ahead.

"And what happened to those on board?" Hannah asked, but she almost did not wish to know the answer. Too many things during the war had been dismissed as being too bad to believe. She didn't want to make the same mistake again.

"The British had an internment camp near Haifa, called Atlit. They were transferred there. But last October, the Palmach broke in and liberated everyone."

Vera sensed Hannah's worry. She hadn't really been asking out of concern for the success of the prior ships, or the workings of Aliyah Bet, the massive movement to bring refugees to Israel. Hannah was concerned for herself and Eli.

She did what she could to reassure Hannah. Vera herself was only a piece in the puzzle, but she knew of those coordinating ships, those raising funds both in Palestine and in America, and of the others who were planning military actions against the British. Even before the war, she knew it was only a matter of time for the Zionist dream to take root.

Vera's mind drifted to the last day she had seen her own mother. She wished it had been a different memory. It had been a cold January day in 1938, one month past her eighteenth birthday. She remembered how her family had stood on the train platform, waving her off, how everyone had been there but for her mother, who had refused. She'd stayed back at the apartment, which had witnessed too many heated arguments between mother and daughter. As Vera left the apartment, her mother had given her a hug, kissed her forehead and then simply turned away to stare out the window. Vera said nothing either as she grabbed her suitcase and walked away.

At fifteen, Vera had insisted she was moving to Palestine, though she knew it was against her parents' wishes. Her mother argued that they had not brought her up in society and sent her to the finest schools, only for her to become a farmworker in rags. Her father had tried a more diplomatic approach, convinced that she would grow out of this idea. He said that, if she would wait until she was eighteen, he would support her choice, even if he didn't understand it. With rumors of war on the horizon, he'd wondered, albeit silently, if they shouldn't all go.

Letters took weeks to arrive, and by the time Vera—and the world—had a better idea of what was occurring, it was too late to get her family out. She'd waited and prayed, but the last she knew was that the family had been taken away, where or when exactly was not clear.

When the clouds of war broke, she returned to try to find her parents, her brother, his wife, her niece...

anyone. What she found instead was beyond words. And so Vera figured that even though she hadn't been able to get her parents out of Europe, she would help as many as she could instead. With the help of an entire network, she began to collect children from DP camps. She registered every child—the best thing anyone could do in the hope that someone was looking for them, but Vera knew it was unlikely.

***

By the third day, Eli had fallen ill. Hannah did what she could to keep him fed and hydrated, but the lulling of the ship showed no mercy. She smiled when she saw how he was clinging to Louise. It had been years since she had seen that stuffed bunny.

Eli was horribly seasick for days on end, and he had convinced himself that he would die before they reached land. The very moment those on board spotted the shore, a cheer went up throughout the ship. Hannah assured Eli they were almost there.

She had convinced Eli to come out on deck, rather than stay in the rancid bowels of the ship, hoping that the sight of the shore would raise his spirits, seeing the image bright and shining in the distance, but then she heard a horn and shouting over the loud speaker. There was a battle ship dangerously close.

The deck was pure chaos; people wailed and screamed in several languages. Someone shouted that they were going to be fired upon. Some on board began to hurl themselves into the sea. Eli was terrified that the boat was sinking, and he didn't know how to swim. He looked at his mother, her eyes fixated on the shore. She was not frantic; rather, she calmly told Eli that the boat was turning back to Europe. Vera did the same to calm her children.

Eli watched those who had thrown themselves into the water attempting to paddle their way to shore, but it was to no avail. The British quickly plucked them from the water and brought them onto the larger vessel. Eli was not sure what would happen to them, but as they thrashed, their bodies attempting to break free, Eli knew that they were not going to the shore. He wept like so many others on board, but for different reasons

DAY ONE IN TURKEY

2015

Safia couldn't rest. She stood there watching Nadir and Asma, curled up in a pile of pillows and blankets. Laia was sleeping on the other side of the children, and Yusef was on the couch, but was lying at an awkward angle as he was too tall for it. Safia slipped out of the room, and the cool spring air hit her. She had not realized how warm the container home was. Her mind replayed the events of the last few days, and she tried to shake away all of the what ifs.

She had finally been able to reach Ahmed, who as she had suspected, was in Syria. He was still in Damascus. He had heard Safia's voicemail when he landed. Not many words were shared, but each other's brokenness was clear across the line. Ahmed insisted on coming to Turkey, but Aida's words stuck in her head. Safia knew that, for most of the people in the refugee camps, they are there for decades, in a proverbial no man's land, unable to move forward and unable to go back. Safia did not want that for her children, not when all they had to do was wait another few months for the entire family to have British visas. She told Ahmed to get out of Damascus and back to London. The conversation turned from sorrowful to furious. Ahmed asserted that he was coming to Turkey, with Safia shouting back that there was nothing he could do there and that if he really wanted to help, he would go back to England. Ahmed kept apologizing, as did she, not so much to one another, but because both blamed themselves for Salim's death.

Safia promised to call Ahmed the following morning. There was more to be decided, and it was too much to go through within just one call. As she sat on the small stoop of the container house, Safia thought about what to do next. The first priority was to get the children registered. And Nadir needed more insulin. She wasn't so worried about housing or food; Ahmed would wire-transfer her any money she needed and a payment was already on the way. He was also working on arranging new bank and credit cards, but that in all would take about a week.

The next morning, Aida helped everyone get registered and, to her relief, Safia was able to get insulin for Nadir. She was also able to receive the money from the wire transfer, as well as the location of the embassy in Istanbul where she would get the new passports. She also applied for Turkish ID cards. Until they had them, they would have to stay in the camp. Technically, they were all in Turkey illegally, until they had the ID cards; apparently those caught traveling without them would be deported back to the Syrian side. Safia was not sure whether this was true or not, but she didn't want to risk it. She hoped they would come soon, as she didn't like being this close to the border, less than a half mile away. Only weeks before, she had seen rockets coming across from Syria.

Container homes were being built as quickly as possible, but until then, everyone would be sleeping on Aida and Muhammad's floor. They didn't seem to mind. By camp standards, both Laia and Safia were extremely wealthy. The women bought a feast for that night, and Safia was finally able to rest. *It will be alright*, she told herself.

Safia was shaken awake by Laia. The darkness disoriented her but she saw the woman put her finger to her mouth to tell her to be quiet. She followed Laia outside.

"Where are we going?" she whispered, though unsure why she was whispering.

"Come with me," Laia said. They weaved through the camp. It was well lit but the maze of houses, which all looked alike, made it feel like a maze.

They entered a house that looked like all the others,

and before she even stepped across the threshold, she could hear a woman crying. The layout was the exact same as every other container house, and they made their way to the backroom, where a young woman was deep in the throes of labor. While Safia didn't quite understand why the young woman was not in the hospital, she jumped in to assist. Advising the other women around her on what to bring and what to do, Safia helped the woman, who she came to learn was called Farah, welcome a beautiful baby boy into the world. As she cradled him, Safia couldn't help but think he looked like Salim.

As the sun rose and the morning light streamed in, she could see Farah's face more clearly, and Safia realized that she couldn't have been more than fourteen or fifteen. One of the older women thanked Safia profusely and pressed money into her palm. Safia refused, and when the women wouldn't take it back, Safia placed it on the counter. She gave some advice to the new mother before she left, saying that she would be back tomorrow to check on both of them. The older woman insisted that would not be necessary and all but pushed Laia and Safia out the front door.
As they walked away from the house, Safia finally broke the silence.

"I don't understand," she said, taking a firm step in front of Laia, preventing her from moving forward.

Laia let out a sigh and stepped around her. "When you registered, word spread that you are a doctor."

"There are plenty of doctors. There is an entire hospital," Safia said, gesturing toward the hospital.

"Keep your voice down," Laia scolded. "Aida has been acting as midwife for months, but she has had no formal training. She told me the entire story, or what she knew of it. There are many reasons that women cannot go to the hospital here."

Safia worried what Laia meant by this.

"Farah is here alone. She is fourteen," Laia continued. "She was the only one from her family who made it from Idlib. Do you suppose that child has a husband?"

"So who is the father?" Safia said, more softly. Laia had once again surprised her with her astuteness.

"She won't say. She is terrified."

"What will happen to them?" she said, wondering more to herself than to Laia.

"The older woman is going to take in the baby as her own. Farah will hopefully be able to grow up and one day marry."

Safia didn't press any further, as more than anything she needed a shower and a cup of coffee, but Farah stayed on her mind for most of that day.

WINTER CAMP

1947

There was confusion when the boat was escorted away from the shore. Little actual information was to be had. Some insisted they would be returned to Europe and each repatriated to the country of their birth. There were those who wept and there who sat silently, frozen in fear. Hannah returned Eli to the bunk beds down below, resigned to the fact that the ship would take them back to France. After the emotional exhaustion and being sick for days on end , Eli collapsed on the bed and was asleep instantly. It was only then that Hannah allowed herself to cry.

By the next morning, however, it was revealed that they would not be returning to France, but headed to an island called Cyprus. The British had decided in August of the prior year that, due to the mass influx, those trying to illegally enter Palestine would be detained in several camps on the island.

Hannah was grateful for dry land, but then she saw the camp. It was surrounded by barbed wire and watch towers. Hannah held Eli close to her, unsure what would happen now. The British were unmoved by the pleas and sobs of the passengers as they were brought into the camp. Tents were set up in what Hannah heard was called "summer camp #60." They stayed huddled together, children behind mothers, waiting to see what would come next.

A friendly looking woman came out to reassure them that they were safe and began to organize the masses into shelters. The camps had been built to house 10,000 people, but by 1947, they were well beyond capacity, with numbers nearer to 16,000. The tent Hannah and Eli were assigned had no furniture except a cot and a kerosine lamp, which would be shared with another woman and her two small children. Eli only remembered being grateful that the cot did not move under him when he slept.

Hannah curled in next to Eli. *We'll face tomorrow in the morning*, she thought.

During the night, the wind of the Mediterranean sea whipped at the sides of the tent. Hannah was quite sure that it would tear free of its ropes, but it did not. The wind was cold and both Hannah and Eli shivered under the thin blanket. At one point, Hannah opened her eyes to see the mother staring back at her, huddling with her two children. No words needed to be exchanged. It would be the first of many nights they would freeze, but still, that was preferable to the unbearable heat of summer.

On the first morning, Hannah stepped out of the tent with Eli to find some food. She still had the meager Francs from Sabine, but something told her they would do her no good. People moved around almost in trance. Finally, she saw a familiar face: Vera. She was chatting in Hebrew almost merrily with a young man. In a camp full of pale, unnourished survivors, some still in the tattered clothing from camps all over Europe, the man was tall, tan and muscular. Hannah couldn't help but think he was handsome. Perhaps it was his youth, but he reminded her of David, even though David was never tall, tan or muscular. He had the same dark, but warm, brown eyes that David had.

Vera introduced Hannah and Eli to Yossi. He, like Vera, was a citizen of Palestine, and, like Vera, was resolved to help survivors. The two of them had every right to return as citizens, but instead they wanted to stay in the camps. Vera would teach the children Hebrew, and Yossi—well—all Hannah could glean was that he would teach other "skills." While Hannah could not be sure, it seemed as if right under the noses of the British, military tactics were being taught to some of the teenage boys.

Vera explained that, while the British were content to run the security of the open air prison, they wanted very little to do with the everyday affairs. Vera went on to explain that, like the friendly woman who had tried to reassure *The Moresby* passengers that they were safe, many Jewish organizations had taken over, attempting to address the needs of those in camps. As long as they made no trouble, they were left to their own devices. Vera had known in Marseille that being interned in a camp was a possible outcome and yet, she still choose to take the trip. Hannah wondered where Vera obtained—and more importantly, retained—such conviction to allow herself to stay in such a camp.

Yet, the rest were still prisoners: unable to go to Palestine, unwelcome and unable to rebuild back in Europe. Everyone wanted out of the camp, as despite the efforts to improve the lives of those living there, conditions were still very poor. By summer, the heat sweltered and there was never enough water. Sanitary conditions were exacerbated by this; infections spread and the doctors could do little to prevent it. When word came that the British would start allowing those in Cyprus to travel legally to Palestine under their quota system, hope returned. But it was only a couple hundred people a month, with thousands still waiting. Pregnant women, orphaned children and the elderly were the first to be allowed to leave.

A month passed and then two. Eli was kept occupied by school and the overwhelming amount of children that he was able to play with, but Hannah had very little to do to pass her days. She often checked with the Search Bureaus for Missing Relatives and the Red Cross, hoping that David was somewhere looking for her. Every time there was no word, another tiny piece of her died inside.

Over the summer, Hannah developed a chronic skin infection, and most days, she had little strength to rise from her cot. She barely ate, and the doctors were convinced if she stayed any longer, she would die. But despite this, she was not moved up the list. In July, Vera and Yossi, who were now engaged, tried every back channel they knew to get Hannah and Eli to the top of the list but to no avail. Babies were being born every day and they took first priority. The camp that had been built for ten thousand, had now seen more than five times that come through.

In the fall of 1947, it seemed as if Hannah had turned a corner; some color had returned to her face and she would often sit in the sun on a stool outside her tent. Word that the UN had passed Resolution 181 to create a Jewish state and an Arab state in Palestine, further lifted her spirits. For the first time in years, Hannah was hopeful.

She was surprised when, finally, after days of fruitless effort, there was a letter for her from the American Red Cross. She first scanned to see if the signature was David's; it was not. She tore it open. She read the letter without breathing.

Mrs. Bronstein,

We regret to inform you that your husband, David Bronstein, was amongst those who died in Auschwitz.

If there was more to the letter, Hannah didn't read it, as her legs collapsed under her. Darkness enveloped her eyes. She sank into the cold mud, but she couldn't feel it. How she made it back to her tent didn't matter either.

Vera, who had become close friends with Hannah, stayed nearby and called for doctor, but after having read the letter, Vera was not sure there was much a doctor could do. Either way, the woman looked especially unwell. Thankfully, Yossi had somehow materialized a football, and was able to keep Eli occupied.

"Eli. He has no one left now." Hannah sobbed.
"Don't talk like that. It won't always be like this. Soon we will have a country of our own."

"He was supposed to meet us there," Hannah said to Vera, but it was a statement that was incoherent to her, a fragment of a story not told.

"All you need to do now is rest." Vera went to brush the hair that had stuck to Hannah's face from the tears. Hannah seemed to be burning up. Vera's suspicion was confirmed when the doctor finally arrived. After checking her over, he motioned to Vera to speak outside. There, she showed him the letter.

"I cannot be sure, but my best guess is some type of infection, which has only worsened by the trauma of today."

"Can you treat it?"

"I gave her antibiotics, but if her fever does not break tonight, she will have to be transferred to the military hospital in the morning."

Hannah Bronstein died that night. The official cause of death was septicemia. Even if the doctor had known this, there was nothing he could have done. She was among the 400 refugees who died in Cyprus and were buried at Margoa cemetery. Eli would always insist that she died of a broken heart. Despite all the evidence, she still believed that David was somehow also on his way to Israel. When that hope died, Hannah's heart simply gave out.

THE FIRST
TWO WEEKS

2015

T he two first weeks in the camp passed quickly, as the family settled into a routine. Ahmed called Safia every day at 8am and every night 6pm, more to hear her voice that to share any news. He had funded her account with more money than she could spend. He did not tell her that he had also sent money to Dr. Tahan for Salim's burial. It had taken two weeks but they had finally located his body within the rubble. Ahmed would tell Safia one day, but not over the phone. The children took turns telling him all about the other kids and the playground. Asma would talk without ceasing until Nadir would chime in, and eventually Safia would have to wrestle the phone from them.

Ahmed was instantly filled with terror when his

phone rang at 3 am Safia's time. She had told him she'd been having nightmares but had never called him in the middle of the night. In the split-second it took to answer his cell, he ran through every worst-case scenario he could think of: another errant bombing had hit the camp, one of the children was sick, Safia was sick, they were being deported.

"Are you okay?" he asked.

"We are okay," she said quietly.

"Oh thank god! I was so worried for a moment." Ahmed exhaled. The line was silent for a moment. "Safia?"

"I am here."

"Talk to me. What is going on?"

"I am scared. It's hard to explain."

"Try, please."

Safia let out a deep breath. "There is something happening in the camp. I keep delivering the babies of babies. Three since I have been here. And no one will say how or why. And now there is a rumor of missing children. Of course, no one knows for sure if they have moved on and the Turkish Red Crescent can hardly keep track of the people who others want to be found. I think there is something horrible happening here. And no one can go to the authorities because they are terrified. I am terrified and—"

Ahmed tried to digest what she was saying but the more she rambled the less she made sense. Ahmed heard her though, but he was more concerned about her, than about any rumors. She hadn't been sleeping, nor had she been able to mourn Salim. He feared she was on the verge of a mental breakdown. For everything she had been through, it was completely understandable.

"Safia, take a deep breath. It will be okay. As soon as you get your ID cards you and the children can go to Istanbul. It shouldn't be much longer. I can meet you there."

"Ahmed, you aren't listening! Children are going missing."

"Safia, do you know that for sure?"

"No, but…"

"I want you to try to sleep. We can talk about this tomorrow. You sound exhausted and I am worried about you."

Perhaps Ahmed was right. Safia knew they were only rumors, but the thought of losing another one of her children had driven her to near hysteria. She knew she sounded irrational, so she promised to try to rest. They would speak again in a few hours.

Ahmed rang his immigration lawyer again. He did not care that it was the middle of the night; he could feel that something wasn't right. Safia had endured bombings, lived in a city under siege and stayed when others fled Aleppo—if she was now scared it was serious. He hadn't told Safia about the lawyer. He didn't want to raise her hopes but he was working on tourists visas for them. The lawyer didn't answer but Ahmed left a voicemail.

The next morning, the conversation was calmer. When Ahmed asked about it, all Safia said was, "little ears," a clear sign that the children were with her and it was a topic that could not be discussed. Instead, they filled the conversation with what they would do together once in Istanbul, including a promise to take Nadir and Asma to the zoo. Both reassured one another it would be soon, once the ID cards were issued. And despite the wait, there was no cause for concern. Turkey was absorbing refugees at an alarming rate. The aid workers couldn't keep up, and neither could the amount of paperwork. They had to remind themselves to be patient.

With no official work and nowhere to go, it seemed the camp's only product was gossip. The rumor was that children would arrive unaccompanied from Syria, following the flow of refugees, eager to make it to safety. Yet, once they registered as unaccompanied they would then go missing. This was, of course, impossible to verify in any concrete way, as no one would know to look for a child if no one knew they were missing. One day the rumor would be of one boy or girl, and the next it would be four. The more the rumor spread the bigger it became. Compounding this was that the camp was not set up to provide for lone children, so they would be transferred to the nearest Provincial Child Protection Directorate. The rumor suggested that ten unaccompanied children would be registered, but only eight would be transferred; either the children were being transferred to a place better equipped to care for them, or it was something much worse.

Safia did not wish to scare her children, but she made it very clear they were to be with an adult at all times. All things considered, they seemed blissfully unaware and happy to play with the other children, something they hadn't been able to do for a long time. A bouncing soccer ball was a constant soundtrack of the camp, and Safia loved to watch them running and playing. But now they would have to be more careful.

Over breakfast, Laia's cell phone rang. She mainly listened, sometimes replying with a simple "yes", and then hung up. Grabbing Safia to the side, she whispered, "We have to go right now."

Safia had become used to being called upon to deliver babies, as the Syrian women trusted her more than the Turkish doctors. Safia in turn liked feeling useful; there was something so hopeful about babies being born under the worst circumstances. But babies rarely make a quick entrance into the world, and Laia's stress on the word "now," was unsettling. Safia kissed both children on the forehead and headed out, the morning sun white washing the camp.

"There is a girl in trouble," Laia said.

"What kind of trouble?"

"I am not sure, but it's bad."

They twisted and turned through the camp, walking as briskly as one could, before Laia began to run.

Safia adjusted the backpack she had been using as a medical bag, and said a silent prayer, something she caught herself doing more often these days. After having to turned around once—something easy to do when all the container homes looked the same—they made their way into a house.

The first thing Safia noticed was that three women were crowded around the bathroom. The ashen looks on their faces did little to dull the adrenaline coursing through her veins.

"I am a doctor," Safia said and the women moved aside wordlessly.

The bathroom floor was covered in blood and, as Laia had said, there was a girl barely conscious sitting on the floor.

"What happened?" Safia shouted at no one in particular.

She didn't wait for an answer as she checked the girl for a pulse. It was there but it was weak. Safia whispered to the girl, telling her that she was going to be fine, but she was not so sure. She examined her and confirmed what she suspected.

"She needs a hospital. She had a perforated uterus, and will require surgery."

The women stood unmoved. Safia told Laia to call for an ambulance, but as Laia began to dial, one of the women reached for the phone and said, "You can't. She is alone and has no ID. They will deport her."

Safia stood up and placed herself between the woman.. "If we don't call, she will die. I don't know what will happen once they know, but if we do nothing this girl has no chance for survival." She nodded to Laia, who was already on the line.

"What is her name?" Safia asked.

"Iman."

"You're going to be okay, Iman." Safia said over and over again.

When the ambulance arrived, Safia offered to go with the girl. The camp hospital was well equipped but this was Safia's specialty. She felt compelled to stay with Iman, even if they would not allow her to scrub in. Clearly the girl needed an advocate. She was involved and would see it through. She kept whispering to the girl, reassuring her that she would be just fine.

The mundane-looking doctor had plenty of questions

for Safia, but the one she couldn't answer was what happened. She had a good guess, but she didn't share it with him. This type of injury was most likely the result of a botched abortion. Likely, he knew this too, but was finding some fun in toying with Safia. Technically, abortion was legal in Turkey, but without an ID card, Iman would have had no access to medical care, not to mention the social hurdles she would face. Safia didn't know if she had done it herself or if the silent women who had called for help had.

When the doctor insisted he didn't need Safia's help, her heart sank. And when surgery was complete, he confirmed what she had feared: instead of even attempting to repair the damage, he had removed her reproductive organs. Once the girl was resting comfortably, Safia left. She could feel her blood boiling. Medical care had saved Iman's life, but nothing had been done to even try to make sure she could have a full life.

When she returned to their container, Laia confirmed what she already knew: it was an abortion gone wrong, but that was all that she would say, although she swore she didn't know if it was self-induced or performed by one of the other women. No one would talk. Safia suspected Laia knew someone who would tell the truth.

The next morning, she went to see Iman. She was still groggy and seemed to be in a lot of pain. Safia was able to get her more pain medicine and sat by her bed while she slept. Iman was small for her age, and was far too young to be in this situation.

She visited again the next day, bringing with her some of Aida's Kubbeh Halab. She treaded carefully when she asked Iman what had happened, promising not to tell anyone. Iman hesitated for a moment, but then began to tell her what had happened.

"After our mother died, my brother and I decided to come to Turkey. He was trying to avoid conscription and he said he wouldn't leave me alone. But on the way, we were stopped by rebels. The first time they beat him pretty bad. They kept going until they were convinced he was not a solider. But then when we were stopped again, he was shot. I stayed with him until he died, but after that, I didn't know what to do. So, I kept on journeying toward the border, and a nice family took pity on me and made me like own of their own. The woman was so kind. She braided my hair and gave me an equal portion of food as her own children. But once we arrived in Turkey, everything changed."

Iman began to cry. Safia held her hand and told her it was okay.

"Once we arrived and tried to register, the woman told the camp staff that I was unaccompanied. She assured me this would be best for me, and I believed her. We were waiting to be transferred to the children's home, as they called it, but a man came to me. I had seen him before when I was registering. He said that the children's home was horrible and that as an orphan I would have a horrible life. He said he wanted to help."

Safia nodded, urging Iman to continue.

"He said we would be married. I protested that I was too young, but he just laughed and said I could stay with his family till I was a bit older. He said if I married him, he would provide for me and that I could quickly become a citizen. So I agreed. He said we would have a triple wedding—the two people who would be our witnesses were also taking wives. There was a judge and even a marriage contract. He said I was the most beautiful bride he had ever seen and we would be happy."

"Were you happy?" Safia asked, even though she knew the answer.

"After the wedding, we didn't go to his family house but to his apartment. He said it was so we could have some privacy. He said it would be okay if we were together as man and wife, and I agreed. We were married, so there was no shame in it, but after a few days he told me to leave. I was very confused. I insisted I was his wife. And he just laughed and laughed. I didn't understand why. He told me the marriage contract was a fake. It was in Turkish so I couldn't read it. He told me to get out and he didn't care where I want. When I told him I was going to go to the police, he slapped me and said that I would be deported—or worse."

"Where did you go?"

"He told me he would bring me back to the camp but that I had better keep my mouth shut. So I went to stay with the same family I had met on the journey. They didn't mind but the woman was confused. She never asked me why I wasn't at the home for the children. She didn't say anything, and it was all okay— until I found out I was pregnant. I went to the man to tell him I was carrying his child but he said he didn't know me. When I got back to where I was staying, the woman said I was evil, but she knew people who could help. But she said once it was done, I would have to leave her home forever. I don't know where I will go now." Tears steadily flowed from her cheeks as she whispered the last part.

"Wait, so the man is still here? You said you told him you were pregnant."

"Yes, Emir works in the administration building. So do the judge and the witnesses."

"And the other wives; you said it was a triple wedding."

"I don't know. I hope they are happier than I have been."

Safia had all the proof she needed: the rumors were true. She shuddered to think of those even younger than Iman who had gone missing. She told Iman that they must go to authorities, but the girl shook with fear. Safia promised her it would be okay, that they would do it together once the girl was recuperated, and she eventually relented. Safia kissed Iman on the forehead as she would one of her own children, and promised to check in on her the next day.

CYPRUS

1948

V era and Yossi fought bitterly over whether they should tell Eli about his father. Vera insisted one trauma was enough, but Yossi thought it better to tell him everything at once.

"Have you no compassion? The child just buried his mother."

"And that is sad, but Eli has an entire life in front of him. He cannot always have one eye on the past and one on the future," he replied calmly.

"We could at least let this news settle."

"And what? Wait till he is settled to start the mourning all over again?"

Vera stood to leave the small tent, but stopped at the threshold, holding open a flap and letting the cold winter air in.

Yossi stood motionless for a moment. "If you are so sure, you be the one to tell him."

"Fine."

Yossi strolled out of the tent with all the confidence he could muster, but once he was beyond Vera's sight, he let his shoulders slump. He had met more orphans than he could count, but this was the first time that he would be there when a child found out their new unfortunate status.

Eli was curled up on the cot he had shared with his mother. He was rubbing the silk part of the stuffed bunny's ear tenderly. Yossi was surprised by how small he seemed at that moment. Eli had always been little for his age, but the sight of his small form on that cot broke Yossi's heart. Those in charge wanted to move Eli into the orphan's camp, but Natasha, who had shared the tent with Hannah and Eli over the last year, said he could stay a few more days. It was the only kindness she had to offer. The tent was the only home he had known in years.

Yossi sat on the edge of the cot.

Eli looked at him with wide eyes. In that moment, Yossi wished he had listened to Vera, but he cleared his throat, twice.

"Eli, listen. You are a very brave boy, and soon you will be a very brave man. And...well, I have to tell you something. The day your mama died, a letter came for her. It said that your papa died during the war."

Yossi watched Eli's face for reaction, or tears. But the boy said nothing. He didn't even flinch.

"Do you understand what I am saying?"

Eli nodded.

Yossi sat uncomfortably, not sure what to do. He shifted nervously. Had Eli descended into a ball of tears, he would have at least known how to handle it. But Eli just sat there, fidgeting with the bunny.

"Will I go back to the orphanage?" Eli asked almost excitedly. "I can see Henri and Jean and Sister Emile."

"No, you will travel to the land of Israel."

"But I don't know anyone there. Who will take care of me?" The confusion was thick in Eli's voice.

"Well, you don't know anyone yet, but you will. It will feel like home in no time."

With that, Eli broke into sobs, throwing his face into the blanket. It wasn't so much sadness as it was fear.

Yossi gently rubbed Eli's back, and stayed there with him until he had cried himself to sleep. Natasha nodded to Yossi to let him know she would keep an eye out.

Yossi wasn't sure what would happen next for Eli— there were children's homes, and he knew some children were going to different kibbutzim around the country, but the actual mechanics were a question better suited for Vera. He wished she had been by his side when he delivered the tragic news. He silently promised himself that he would never quarrel with her again.

***

Vera was force to be reckoned with. She pushed and pushed until Eli was moved up the list of those getting a legal certificate to travel to Palestine. There were only 750 visas per month, but she was determined, and in January of 1948, the time came for him to leave. Vera helped Eli pack. Without Hannah's few belongings, the suitcase he and Hannah had brought with them was nearly empty, so a knapsack was found. Into it, Vera placed the few family photos and the couple of letters, including the one from the Red Cross, gingerly bundled together with twine.

Vera and Yossi hugged Eli goodbye and promised they would see him soon, but both were determined to stay at the camp until it closed, until they were no longer needed. Eli said goodbye in Hebrew, the word softened by his French accent. A year in the camp school had prepared him at least in that way.

Arrangements had been made through *Youth Aliyah*: Eli would join a children's village that was run by a kibbutz outside of Haifa.

The ship taking him to Palestine was nothing like *The Moresby*. It was a British freighter ship, twice its size.

It was clean and devoid of the chaos that remained in Eli's mind from the last crossing. The sailors on board were occupied by their duties, and the camp was too far from shore to wave to, so as soon as they boarded, the passengers settled into the area designated to them, a hastily constructed room on the deck surrounded by an enclosure. This was the same ship that had transported the "prisoners" to Cyprus.

Eli spent the journey with another boy, Leo, the two of them getting into mischief together. They would sneak out of the designated area through a small gap in the caging until an annoyed sailor would return them with a scolding. The longer they could explore the ship without being caught the better. Finally, a naval officer told the adults to "mind their children," and an elderly passenger stepped forward and grabbed both boys by the shoulders, nodding solemnly at the officer as he did so. Once the officer's back was turned, the old man winked at the boys and told them to go have fun—just not to get caught again.

Unlike the prior voyage, when the lights of the shore came into view, there was no doubt that they would be able to dock. Many of the passengers cried and rushed onto the deck to watch the shore come into view. The January wind was biting as Eli 's fingers wrapped around the wire enclosure. He closed his eyes and promised himself he would be brave, just as Yossi had told him to be.

It would be an easy date to remember. January 3rd,

1948 was also Eli Bronstein's eleventh birthday.

IMAN

2015

I man was gone. Safia shouted at the nurse and then at the doctor. Besides the concern of her being missing from the hospital, there was no way she was ready to be medically cleared.

The doctor tried to calm her. "Her brother came to bring her home!"

"She doesn't have a brother!" she screamed at him.

"They knew each other." The doctor shrugged and then walked away.

Safia sat down and held her head in her hands. She wanted to cry, but the tears would not flow. Iman wasn't her daughter, but it felt like she had failed to protect yet another child. There was no way of knowing where Iman was or who she was with. She could have been deported, or in jail, or anywhere. Safia knew there would be no locating her and the desperation hit her like a wave.

She collected herself, and walked silently out of the hospital, the world around her muted as she was lost in her own thoughts. She could go to the authorities, but all she had was second-hand knowledge.

Coming around the corner, she could see Asma and Nadir playing. It provided a little comfort to her soul. Yusef was nearby with a friend keeping watch over them. Safia smiled when he caught her watching him from a distance. Yusef was so much like a big kid. He would often happily join in Asma and Nadir's games.

Safia thanked him for keeping an eye on them and then nodded to his friend by way of introduction. "This is Emir," he said nonchalantly.

"Nice to meet you, Emir. Where are you from?"

Yusef laughed. "No, he isn't Syrian. He is Turkish. He works in the administration building."

A chill ran through Safia then. She knew this was the same Emir. She knew it in her soul. It wasn't a coincidence that this morning Iman was missing, and now this man had found Safia. She did the best she could to show no emotion, but she could feel cold sweat on the back of her neck.

Emir was older than she had thought, maybe mid-thirties. He had a slim build and, in every way, reminded Safia of a snake.

Yusef, who was oblivious to the situation, continued on. "Yeah, we got to chatting this morning. He said that ID cards are backlogged for months, but he may be able to help us pull some strings. I told him how we are all looking to get out of here, and your plan on going to Istanbul soon."

In that moment, Safia wanted to strangle Yusef. It wasn't his fault, really; he didn't know. Emir grinned. Safia had no choice but to play along.

"That is very kind of you, Emir."

"I try to help where I can."

Safia was done with this charade. She called Asma and Nadir to finish playing. Nadir begged for a few more minutes, shouting out, "Yusef promised he would kick the ball with us!"

Emir chuckled. "Yusef, you better make good on that promise."

At that, Yusef sprinted over to the children, and playfully stole the ball from Asma.

Emir saddled up closer to Safia. "Cute kids."

She turned to face him, all ready to scream in his face, but Emir cut her off.

"It would be a shame if you were deported or ended up in jail. What would happen to *them*? I heard you have been performing illegal abortions. That's a crime here in Turkey. Don't worry, I know someone who could look after them, especially that Asma."

"Don't threaten me. I know what you've done."

"I would suggest you and your brats leave and go back to Syria. I think you've overstayed your welcome."

Safia stared at him. They both knew that to go back to Syria would be certain death.

"If you don't leave, I will have the Turkish authorities issue a warrant for your arrest. There won't be anywhere in this country safe for you, not even Istanbul. Do you understand?"

He flicked his cigarette and turned to walk away. "Oh, before I forget, you'll be needing this." He placed a vial of insulin in Safia's hands.

She ran over to her children and grabbed each of their small hands, dragging them back to Aida's house. Laia took one look at her and asked, "What has happened?"

Safia ran to her quarters and began throwing every belonging they had into a bag.

"What happened?" Laia tried again.

"We are not safe here. We have to go right now."

"Go where? Slow down. You aren't making any sense."

"Laia, they are going to issue a warrant for my arrest, for performing abortions. Iman is gone—dead or deported, I don't know—and they know who my children are. We have to leave right now."

"They who? You didn't perform any abortions."

"I don't know, but the rumors are true about the missing children. I was going to go with Iman to report what was happening but she is gone."

"Where are you going to go? You don't have ID cards for you or the children. If you get caught leaving the camp without one, you will be deported."

"It's better if you don't know my plan. Now, listen to me, Laia. There is a man named Emir who works in administration. Keep as far away from him as possible."

"Safia, don't go, I beg you. It's too dangerous."

"I have no choice."

And with that, she gathered her bag and grabbed Asma and Nadir. As they headed across the camp, both children asked more questions than Laia. She told them to be silent, hissing at them harsher than she intended to.

The missing children were not the only rumor in the camp. There was also a rumor of a smuggler who could get you out, as well as a whole network of smugglers who could then transport you to anywhere in the country and—most importantly—to a different country entirely.

Her cell phone rang. She didn't recognize the number,

but answered anyway. She was greeted by a female voice. "Hello, this is Miray from administration. We had a couple of questions about your paperwork. Can you come in—"

Safia immediately hung up.

Once she made it to the smuggler's house, she paid the fare for her and the children. They were to leave once night fell. She made one call to Ahmed—he didn't answer; he must have been in surgery.

"Ahmed, I can't say much but the children and I are leaving. Don't call this number. I will call you when I get a new one. I love you so much."

And with that, Safia threw the phone to the ground and crushed it under the heel of her shoe. She knew it was a touch of paranoia, but the adrenaline had taken over.

KIBBUTZ

1948-1955

T here was a great commotion as they docked, but this time it was only excitement that flooded the crowd. Once Eli was processed after landing in Haifa, he was handed over to a young couple who were waiting for another child from the boat, a girl named Chaya. Eli had been so occupied, playing with Leo, that he hadn't met the little blonde-headed girl on the boat. But he did remember the first time he saw her in Haifa, and would do so for the rest of the life. She was the most beautiful thing he had ever seen.

If Eli was shy, Chaya was all but mute. She reminded him of a butterfly: beautiful but supremely fragile. She had been born in Poland and had lost her entire family. How she had managed to survive was not something one asked or discussed, but like any other child who survived, it could only be due to the kindness of strangers. She had spent most of her young life trying to be invisible. It was a skill—or perhaps a curse—she would carry with her her whole life. She spoke almost no Hebrew and looked always like she was scared.

The couple who were to take them to the children's home Sam and Talia, were friendly, and they explained that they would stay the night in the city with a friend before driving up to the kibbutz in the morning. What the children hadn't been told was that the roads were dangerous at night; snipers lay in wait. Since the UN passed resolution 181, the country had been a tinderbox. For the last month, there had been bombings by the Jewish paramilitary group, the Irgun, in both Jaffa and Jerusalem. Only three days before the children arrived, the Irgun had thrown two bombs into a group of Arab laborers in Haifa, killing six and wounding forty-two. In response to this, the Arabs raided the oil refinery killing forty-one Jews. The city—the entire country in fact—was ablaze with such violence; a group would attack, only to be followed by endless retaliations.

As Sam and Talia explained the plan for the night, Chaya nodded along to what she didn't understand, following Eli's lead. Both children were fed, bathed and given pajamas, and Talia brushed and braided Chaya's hair, subtly checking for lice. Chaya was a year younger than Eli, and even to Talia she seemed fragile. She secretly wondered how Chaya would fare on the kibbutz; life could be tough for everyone, let alone someone as innocent as she.

In the morning, both children were treated to breakfast. Both children grinned with delight when waffles and syrup appeared at the table. Compared to the food in Cyprus, it was a proper feast.

The kibbutz sat at the base of Mount Carmel, and when they arrived, Eli shuddered at the fencing. The young man who was driving them explained that it was to keep them safe, but anyone was free to leave at any point. They were free here, and no one's prisoner. Any day now, they would have a country of their own.

Communal living was at the heart of everything on the kibbutz, and the children were brought to the children's home, where all of the children were raised, orphan or not. Those with parents would visit them a few hours in evening.

On that very first morning, Eli met Ben.

Ben was everything Eli was not. Even though Ben was only a year older than Eli, he was a full head taller. Eli was pale and shy, whereas Ben was an outgoing daredevil, tanned from long days in the sun. He was a Sabra; his family had been in Palestine for three generations and Ben wore this like a badge of honor. He was the ring leader in the children's home, and Eli followed him around everywhere. Ben relished this attention.

It was Ben who gave Eli the tour of the kibbutz, the fields that grew olives and lemons, the communal dining hall, and the laundry where dozens of women folded massive piles of material. He also showed Eli the dairy barn, the machine shop and the library. The smell of the books reminded Eli of his father, who has been a bookbinder. When Ben took Eli up the side of the mountain, with Chaya in tow, he was able to show them the entire kibbutz. The children had free run of the massive kibbutz. It was a freedom Chaya and Eli had never known. It was here, with thanks to Ben, that they learned how to be children once more.

From day one, the three of them were inseparable. If you were looking to find one of them, you only need look for the other two. Occasionally, Chaya and Eli would even spend time with Ben's parents during visiting hours. Ben's mother, who had only two sons, doted on Chaya, seeing her as the daughter she never had, but both parents were equally as kind to Eli.

When Israel was established on May 14, 1948, Eli remembered dancing with Chaya and Ben. The children watched as the adults hugged and wept, but for the children, there was nothing but merriment.

But when war was declared the next morning, the merriment was replaced by fear. The battle had raged beyond the border of the kibbutz, with even more bombings, but with the declaration of war, a new fear took hold. The kibbutz, like everywhere else, mobilized; every able-bodied man—and a few teenagers who found themselves suddenly a year or two older than their birth certificates stated they were—took up arms; food was rationed to be sent to the troops; and everyone waited. News of victories was widely told; news of defeats was whispered, though no news remained secret for long on the kibbutz. The news of other kibbutzim being raided and attacked sent shivers down everyone's spines. Everyone but Ben, that was. Ben lamented being too young to fight, and he insisted that, despite only being twelve, he was almost a man.

During the war, the kibbutz fared better than others. There had been a few times where everyone was packed into bomb shelters, fearing for their life, or when the smoke from Haifa could be seen, but fortunately, when the war ended in March of 1949, those who had remained on the kibbutz were no worse for wear. Ben's older brother who had left to fight returned a hero. To Eli and Ben, his stories were the epic tales of good and evil.

After the war, life became somewhat normal. Days were filled with school and simple chores, but with plenty of time to explore and play games. They were limited only to what their imagination could come up with, and rarely, boredom would get the better of them. One such time that both boys—and by association, Chaya—landed in trouble, was after a kumquat fight. The myth of how it started changed over the years with whomever told the story and when, but the fact was the boys plucked the tiny citrus from the tree and spent a good amount of time throwing them at one another. When it was over, the boys had plucked the tree bald, smelled like citrus and had given each other welts all over. It was the teacher, not Ben's parents, who handed out the punishment. This was also a part of the story changed by whomever told it, but all confirmed it was the most trouble they had ever been in.

Eli and Ben, like true brothers, loved to compete with one another over everything, Ben often beating Eli on physical pursuits, while Eli won every academic contest. Chaya, still quiet, but having mastered Hebrew, began to become more outspoken and often found herself as the moderator between the two boys.

There were summers spent at the pool, breaks from school, picking olives, and taking turns milking the cows, always with their eyes on the future. In the summer of 1954, Ben was to leave the kibbutz to begin his mandatory military service. Eli would go the following year, and then Chaya the year after that. Making the most of their last few days of freedom, they headed to Tel Aviv, with their three days off from their "jobs," on the kibbutz, and a train fare in hand. A distant cousin of Ben's, a strange skittish man in his late 40s who was always adjusting his glasses, let them stay. Still they were grateful. Tel Aviv felt like another planet compared to the kibbutz.

Eli would remember this Tel Aviv trip as the last good time spent as a trio. Their days were spent at the beach, playing matkot for hours on end. Nights were spent walking along the boulevards, with ice cream in hand. Restaurants were scarce due to shortages and beyond their budget anyhow. Instead, they would walk around aimlessly. Chaya would stand, looking in shop windows at dresses and hats, only to bemoan her own. The true excitement came on their last night in Tel Aviv, when they procured cinema tickets to see "How to Marry a Millionaire."

Back on the kibbutz, one more party was thrown before Ben headed off. Musicians played folk music and the summer air was soft. It was the perfect night. Chaya wore a green dress that, like all the clothes on the kibbutz, had once belonged to someone else, but Eli and everyone else could see how stunning she looked. When the band announced that they had one more song before calling it a night, Ben insisted on the last dance. Eli thought nothing of letting him cut in —it was his party after all—but Eli watched tensely as Ben held Chaya a little too close, and then felt the sting of jealousy when he leaned in for a kiss.

Eli stormed off, confused by his own anger. Chaya was like a sister to him, and he had never thought of her as anything other than that until that moment when he saw Ben kissing her. But Eli had loved her since the first time he had seen her. The worst part, Eli thought as he sat in the damp grass, was that he didn't even know why he was so angry. Ben didn't know he was in love with Chaya. Besides, he would be leaving in the morning for three years of service.

That first year with Ben away was once of the best of

Eli's entire life. He and Chaya had become closer than ever. They spent nearly every afternoon together. Without Ben, the atmosphere had changed, from the trio getting into mischief to something more adult-like. On the weekends, they would climb the mountains surrounding the kibbutz, talking about anything and everything. Eli was still on the fence over what he wanted to do after his military service, whereas Chaya didn't care much about what she "did." She only wanted to be a wife and a mother. Eli asked her how many children she wanted, and she declared "at least five." Neither had plans to stay on the kibbutz and become members. Eli was more drawn to academia, and Chaya wanted to raise her babies herself. She also noted she wanted a small cottage by the sea with her own garden, so that she could grow flowers simply to look at, asking nothing of them but to be beautiful.

One day, while sitting on a rock, overlooking the valley below, Chaya asked Eli if he would ever go back.

"Go back where?"

"Europe. France."

Chaya had broken an unspoken rule. The past was simply not discussed. Eli recalled Yossi, before he left Cyprus, telling him to only ever look forward, that trying to look to both the past and the future was like your eyes pointing in different directions. But Chaya knew what Ben and the others could never understand: the unexplainable need to go "home."

"Yeah, one day. I hardly remember Paris. Not sure I could even find the apartment. But the address might be in a small batch of letters and stuff I have."

Eli had never opened the packet that Vera had tied for him, of the letters and photos. One day he would look, he often told himself, but that day never came.

"Will you ever go back to Poland?" Eli asked.

"No. There is nothing there for me," she said, her tone ending the conversation as quickly as she had started it.

Ben would visit for a week, here or there, while he was on leave. It was almost like old times but not quite. For the competition between the brothers now had the highest stake of all: the love of Chaya. When Ben first left, he would write to Chaya and Eli, sending them a single, joint letter. But as time went on, his letters came only addressed to Chaya.

And then, it was Eli's turn to enlist. His party was a little bit more subdued that Ben's—for all the talk of equality on the kibbutz, there were always subtle reminders that he was not a natural-born son—but still, there was music and dancing. He and Chaya danced all night, laughing and reminiscing about their antics. Ben had tried to get leave, but Eli was happy when he told him that he couldn't make it. Ben, whether he meant to or not, overshadowed Eli in almost every way. And that night, Eli didn't want to compete with anyone.

Eli went to sleep that night kicking himself, for he had not kissed Chaya. He rose very early to catch the bus, and as he left, walking toward the gates that had made him shudder as a child, he could still smell the dew that hung in the air. .

Just as he was about to leave for good, he heard Chaya call his name.

When Eli turned around, Chaya's nerves failed her and all she said was, "be careful." But Eli was not going to make the same mistake twice. He dropped his bag, took her in his arms, and gave her the kiss he should have the night before.

SAFIA TAKES FLIGHT

2015

B y the time Ahmed was able to reach Laia, Safia and the children were gone. Laia couldn't explain what had happened because she didn't quite comprehend it herself. All she could tell him was what he already knew. She had been terrified for the children so she left. It was a dangerous proposition trying to cross Turkey without documentation, but what Ahmed didn't know was that the market for moving refugees across Turkey was well coordinated.

In the back of the van that evening, while Asma and Nadir slept, Safia watched the street lights as they whizzed past in quick succession. Since Salim passed, she had hardly slept. She always felt like she needed to keep watch. Her transportation was a variable underground rail road which took you wherever you wanted to go. All of the "cabbies" as they called them-selves knew one another, and would send messages about police or advise on friendly rest stops—though most in Turkey were friendly if you kept to yourself. The best part was they asked no questions; they took your money and took you where you wanted to go. Safia struggled on this in particular. She didn't know where she wanted to go. It would have been easiest to blend in and disappear in a major city like Istanbul, but that plan was now no longer possible. All the legal channels had been closed to her.

After several stops, the cabbie gave her a look as if to say "where to next?." It was the end of his route and he could only help her find a new one if he knew where she wanted to go.

"Assos," she half whispered.
Why a Syrian would head to Assos was the least well-kept secret in all of Turkey. It was the crossing point to Greece. Earlier in the year, the EU and Turkey had passed a law, saying that any Syrian who crossed the Aegean to Greek soil was given protected status. The cabbie nodded and gestured to a minivan on the other side of the parking lot. There were already several people gathered around, shifting uncomfortably, but the cabbies were in no rush to finish their cigarettes, as they passed around a thermos of coffee.

"I am hungry," Asma said, bleary eyed.

Safia, who had taken every piece of fruit when she left, leaving money on the counter after grabbing what she could carry, handed Asma an apple. Nadir then wanted one as well. The children ate in silence until the driver called out, "Yalla."

There were more people than seats, but Safia put Nadir on her lap and let him drift back to sleep. Hours passed and when they finally stopped, Safia could smell the salt of the sea. The smell took her back to the last time they had gone to the beach as a family. She wished she had known then how perfect that day was.

Shuffling out of the van with the others and exchanging questioning looks, they looked to the driver for guidance, and he gestured to an unremarkable house, indicating that they should follow him. He smiled, trying to relieve them of their worries. No one spoke. It was still the early hours of the morning.

Once in the house, a boisterous man came forward and hugged the cabbie, exchanging some pleasantries. The man was more round that he was tall, but he had a contagious laugh. Finally, he turned to the group and introduced himself. "I am Ibrahim," he said. "This is my home. You are most welcome here." No one moved. "Please, please, come sit and relax," he said, gesturing that they follow him further into the home. Tea and coffee was produced and the tension began to fade. Everyone relaxed when he went on to say, "I was born in Turkey, but my wife is Syrian."

Ibrahim went on to explain that while he knew most would try the ocean crossing, no one was obligated to and were welcome to stay as long as it took to make other arrangements. The way he said it made Safia stomach drop. It didn't take a genius to understand what he was telling them. The ocean was dangerous.

"Should you need anything, my wife Rabia or my daughter will be happy to help in any way we can." It all felt a little too good to be true. Safia knew the Turkish people were known to be friendly, but this was something else. However, she had no choice but to trust him, though she stayed guarded all the same.

After tea was cleaned up, the road-wary group was shown to small but tidy bedrooms. After settling Asma and Nadir, Safia approached the older woman who she guessed was Ibrahim's wife, Rabia. She pulled the almost empty vial of insulin from her bag and asked the woman if she could get more from the pharmacy. The woman stared at Safia with pity, and patted her cheek gently. "Of course," she said.

"May I take this to show them?" she said, reaching out for the vial.

"Of course, but please be very careful with it. It is the last of it I have."

"I understand."

Safia hoped she could trust this woman. "One more thing, how do I get a new cell phone?"

"I can help with that as well. If you give me the money, I will purchase one while I am out. Please understand you are our guest, not our prisoner. You can go out in the day for small errands but nothing that will raise attention to you. Do you speak any Turkish?"

"No." Safia shook her head. She could understand key pieces but speaking it was a different story, and something that would certainly draw attention.

"Then best let me do your shopping. Both countries are trying to cut down on people trying to cross."

Safia handed her more money than she would need, and Rabia swiftly pocketed it. She winked at Safia and told her to rest. She would go in the morning to get what was needed.

***

Safia woke unable to remember where she was. She'd slept so hard, she was dizzy from waking. When she didn't see Asma or Nadir, panic washed over her and she sprung to her feet, calling their names.

"We are out here," a singsong voice called out a couple of times from another spot in the house.

Weaving her way through the rooms, following the voice, she finally saw Asma and Nadir. They were with a young woman in the small plot at the back at the house. The space was closed in on three sides, and on the fourth was what appeared to be a small vegetable garden, as well as a spot to hang laundry. The children were both laughing at a small kitten which was playing by their feet, as they took turns dangling a piece of string.

The woman smiled. "We didn't mean to startle you. You were sleeping so soundly—thought these two would like some fresh air."

"Look, Mom!" Nadir exclaimed as the kitten wrapped itself up in the string. It was crying loudly to display its displeasure.

"I am Emine," the woman said, as she began to carefully unwrap the kitten from its strong prison. "But people call me Emi. My mother was looking for you. She is in the kitchen."

Safia reached out to grab Asma and Nadir's hands, but Emi told her it would be okay if they stayed; she would keep an eye on them. Safia hesitated for a moment, but she could tell that Emi was a gentle soul.

Once in the kitchen, Rabia insisted Safia eat, laying a plate of eggs and vegetables in front of her. It was as if Rabia was doing ten things at once: cooking, cleaning and occasionally shouting at her other daughter to do this or that. It was flurry of activity. But between the family of four and then eight travelers, there were a lot of people in one tiny house.

When Rabia finally sat down, it was only momentary, as she was straight back up again. "I almost forgot," she said as she produced a cell phone from her bag. She then went to the fridge, pulled out a small vial and handed it to Safia. "I am sorry. I didn't know if it had to be kept cold, but I figured better safe than sorry." Safia was speechless, but it didn't matter as Rabia was still speaking as she bustled about. "You gave me too much money."

And then she laid Safia's change on the table. The kindness overwhelmed Safia and she burst into tears, which then turned into uncontrollable sobs. Rabia cradled her as she cried. "It's okay, you are safe. " Rabia had seen enough people come through her home with trauma so unspeakable, she was not unnerved one bit by Safia's tears. Once the tears stopped, she sat with Safia in silence.

"I am so sorry," Safia finally said.

"Hush, I cannot imagine what you and those babies have been through." She gestured toward the back plot.

"I have to call my husband."

That grabbed Rabia's attention. Until now, she has assumed that Safia was a widow. "Is your husband still in Syria?"

"No, he is in London. He went ahead to get visas."

"If you have visas, what are you doing here?"

"We don't have visas. He is working on it, but I have no passports."

"Oh, well. You can get passports in Istanbul..." Rabia trailed off as her confusion grew.

"I can't," Safia said.

Rabia nodded as if she understood, but she didn't. She grabbed Safia's hand and looked her dead in the eyes in a way that made Safia want to retreat into herself. "Listen to me, I don't know what you've done or why you are here, but promise me you will not do what you are thinking."

Safia nodded. And then excused herself to call Ahmed.

Ahmed was waiting for the call. He didn't know where Safia or his children were. The visas were tied up in paperwork. With nothing else to do but wait, he had punched a hole through the dry wall. A man not usually prone to violence, he was so consumed in his anger he surprised himself. It was anger at everything —at the rebels, at the world, but mostly at himself. He was a husband and a father; he had only one job: to protect them.

He didn't recognize the number on the screen, but he knew instinctively it was her.

"Safia? Safia? Is it you? Where are you? Wherever it is, I am coming to you!" he said before she even answered.

Despite the kindness that Ibrahim and Rabia had showed her, Safia didn't want them to hear what she needed to say. Kindness would only extend so far, and having a fugitive in your home was something entirely different. So, she had taken the children down to the beach to call Ahmed. The children played happily as she began to recount what had transpired.

Ahmed tried to listen without interrupting her, but he could hear in her voice that something was off. The fear was palpable as she explained what had happened. He could hear the wind off the sea in the background, making her voice sound even smaller and further away.

"I am sure they were only trying to scare you. Istanbul will be safe. It's too large a city; they won't find you. I could be on a plane tonight."

"But what if the police are looking for me?!" Safia snapped back. She was frustrated that Ahmed wasn't listening to her.

"Safia, there is no one looking for you. It was only to scare you. Think about it: if they are doing what you said they are, there is no way they would involve the police. There is no order for your arrest."

"But what if there is?"

Ahmed could sense he was losing this battle, so he shifted the conversation. "I will be on flight tonight. Where exactly are you? Are you near Assos or in Assos? Do you have an address?"

"NO!" Safia cut him off.

Ahmed was startled. Safia had never been this short-tempered before.

"Did you get new passports for the children and me?"

Safia asked. She was sounding more and more agitated as the call went on.

The plan for the passports had been to go to Istanbul to try to get them. The tourist visas that the lawyer had promised them—and that were apparently only a matter of days away—required them to have passports first. Ahmed had spent days at the embassy in London, paying a small fortune to have them issued.

"They will be ready a week or so from today."

Safia tried to sound calmer. She knew that she hadn't been sleeping, and besides the breakfast from Rabia, she couldn't remember the last time she ate. Since losing Salim, it had all been a bit of a haze. She wondered if he was still there under the rubble, if he was scared being alone. She could almost hear him crying.

"Safia? Are you there?" Ahmed repeated himself three or four times before Safia was able to pull herself away from her thoughts to answer.

"When you have the passports, we will meet you in Istanbul," she said. "The only place I am going in Istanbul is the airport, do you understand?"

"I do, but—"

"Ahmed, I cannot discuss it anymore. You were not there. And the reason why you weren't there for us was because you were supposed to be getting us visas! You didn't see! And now you don't want to see. You want to come see us and then leave again and then what?"

Ahmed was speechless. He knew he blamed himself for not being with his family, but it had never occurred to him that Safia would too.

"I am sorry. I have to go," Safia said abruptly. "I will call you tomorrow." With that, she hung up the phone.

HAIFA

1956-1958

Without either Eli or Ben, Chaya now struggled on the kibbutz. For the first time since emigrating, she was scared and alone. She retreated back into herself. She told herself over and over again that both would be fine, but she couldn't help but replay the fragmented memories of when she had left her parents. She wondered if that was how it had occurred in real life or if her heart had designed a different, easier image for her to cling on to. She had only been three years old when she was smuggled out of the ghetto, and in her scattered memory, she remembered the rough flannel of her father's coat scratching up against her face as he embraced her one last time. Her mother's face was harder to see, no matter how many times she tried, but what she did remember was how even then, her tiny heart ached for her family. Now, she felt the same ache for Eli and Ben, her new family in the new land she had made her home.

Chaya was set to begin her own military service in the winter, but with the amount of stress she was under, Chaya was given a medical deferment. The paperwork stated that it was due to a "nervous breakdown." It was all suddenly too heavy to bear, and everyone agreed it best that she stay on the kibbutz until she regained her strength. It was as if by finally stopping, the past had caught up to her. But it felt wrong to bring up her history when immediate survival was the goal.

She hadn't needed to worry. Ben had taken to the army as well as his older brother. This surprised no one; nor did the fact that Eli struggled. Both were in the Golani brigade, albeit stationed on opposite ends of the country.

Eli was assigned to an armored brigade as tank loader, while Ben was part of the 51st first assault infantry. That year, during the Suez canal crisis, Eli had been sitting and sweltering in the tank on the relatively peaceful Jordanian border while Ben was helping to capture the heavily fortified city of Rafah. By capturing Rafah, the Egyptians were cut off from Gaza, and the Sinai which was under Israeli control.

Eli was the first to take leave and make it back to the kibbutz. Chaya had kept her letters pleasant and light but the mere fact that she had not yet enlisted told him that something wasn't right. When he saw her, it was as if someone had turned the light off—you could look her in the eyes but not really see her. Over the few days while he was home, she started improving, but he had no idea whether she would continue to. He hated to leave again, but was due back at his base. Knowing that Ben was due home soon, brought him some comfort.

When it was his turn to return home, Ben saw what Eli had seen, and in their letters, the only topic seemed to be Chaya. Eli thought she should leave the kibbutz. Ben, on the other hand, wrote back that the kibbutz was the only safety net there was for Chaya. Anywhere else she went, she would not be part of someone else's family. Evidently, Ben couldn't really understand what it was like to be among people but not really one of them.

One thing was apparent to both men, was that both were in love with her.

***

Chaya had been doing better since seeing both of the boys. She had also been given a role in the kindergarten, a role she much better enjoyed than working in the communal dining hall. Ben, who had been due to end his military service in 1957, had decided to make a career of it, and was steadily working his way up the ranks. Eli, on the other hand, had only one thing on his mind. He wrote to Chaya in January of 1958, after writing and rewriting the letter for weeks on end.

Chaya,
Yesterday was my birthday. Thank you for the

letter you sent.

In all the birthdays I have had in my twenty years on this earth, the only one that is special to me is the one in 1948. You may not have remembered, but that was the day we docked in the port of Haifa. Perhaps it was double birthday. The day I was born and the day I first saw you. I had hoped to have leave to ask the question I want to ask, but every time I see your green eyes my tongue ceases to work.

Will you marry me? I know I am a poor man, but I promise I will spend my life making sure you have everything you deserve and I promise not to punish our five children when they throw kumquats at one another.

With Love,
Your Eli

Eli vibrated with nervous energy as he waited for the reply. *Should I have waited and asked in person?* he wondered. A month passed with no word, so he sent another letter, not asking about the first, but letting her know he would be on leave for Purim in March. Still, he hoped to have word back before then.

March arrived with no word, and for a moment Eli debated even returning to the kibbutz, but his nervousness had turned to anger that she had not responded. He at least deserved an answer. All that righteous indignation melted when he saw Chaya waiting by the gate.

Eli could hardly recall the words she said, but in August Chaya was marrying Ben. She had wanted to tell him in person. Eli tried to remind her that as a career military man she would never see him, nor did she want her children to be raised by others on the kibbutz. What about the house by the sea? Or her flower garden?

"Why him?!" He demanded an answer.

"He loves me."

"I love you!" he said, his voice cracking.

Gossiping on a kibbutz is like an unofficial past time, but the love triangle between Chaya, Ben and Eli sent the mill into overdrive. Everyone had an opinion or a theory. Some said Chaya was pregnant, so she had to marry Ben; others said Eli was her true love and it was due to her nervous breakdown that she wasn't thinking straight. The only answer Eli ever received from Chaya was that Ben made her feel safe and he had asked first.

Two very important things happened that August: Eli finished his military service, and he watched Ben and Chaya get married. It was important for both of them that he was there, and so he stood there watching his best friend marry the love of his life, while his own heart broke.

The next day, he grabbed the same knapsack he had left Cyprus with and the meager savings from his military stipends, and left the kibbutz. He wished Chaya and Ben well, but he didn't need to be there to see it.

For a while, he traveled all over the country, staying with various friends he had met in the army. He was more than restless; he was aimless, lost even.

One night, while staying in Jerusalem with a friend, he pulled out the package from Vera as well as a slightly worse-for-wear Louise. He wondered if he looked as tattered as that poor stuffed bunny. Hadn't they been through the exact same thing? He had been looking forward for so long that maybe he thought it was time to look backwards.

AHMED GOES TO TURKEY

2015

When he couldn't reach Safia, Ahmed began to worry. They never went more than two days without hearing from one another. The line rang so many times, he could almost hear the ringing in his head. On the third day, after the flight to Istanbul, he started first at the embassy and then at the refugee administration. Neither had any record of Safia. He replayed the last call over and over in his head. Had he missed what she was trying to tell him? The only clue he had was the massive amount of money she had withdrawn five days before, each credit card having been used at an ATM in Assos.

Ahmed took the short flight to Assos, unable to control the sick feeling that had taken control of his entire body. It could be as simple as her having misplaced her phone, or that… well, he couldn't think of another reason, but he was sure that there had to be one.

Assos was lovely, it being so far removed from the tragedies that were happening around it. It felt like the beauty was mocking Ahmed. In the old port, boats bobbed up and down, looking like a postcard. Here too, he tried the refugee administration, and unlike the kind gentlemen had in Istanbul, the woman didn't even look at the picture that he showed her. She knew that, if that the smiling woman and her children had been here, it would have only been to cross to Greece.

Desperate and out of options, he sought out the police. He remembered what Safia had said about an arrest warrant. Though unlikely, could she have been arrested? It would at least explain her disappearance. The police were sympathetic but they too had no record of Safia. When Ahmed asked if they could see if there was an arrest warrant out for her, their eyes went wide. They obliged, though, and confirmed what Ahmed had already known: there was no record of Safia anywhere in Turkey's police database.

As he was getting ready to leave, a sergeant asked, "Is it possible she attempted to go to Greece?"

Ahmed shook his head, but he couldn't be sure of anything anymore. He walked to the beach and sat on the sand, wondering if this was the same spot that Safia had called from when he could hear the waves in the distance.

He pulled the photo out of his wallet. He stared at it for a moment, before getting up and asking every person who passed by whether they had seen her. The desperation in his voice produced many sad stares, but they all shook their heads and kept on about their business. The light began to fade, but still Ahmed asked everyone, even when he had to stand under the street light for others to see the image.

A man looked for a moment and said, "Come back here about 4am, and try with the smugglers."

Ahmed looked perplexed. He knew that boats were taking people illegally, but he assumed that the point they left from would be in some cove up the shore, not on the central beach.

He found a hotel room, but he didn't sleep. Instead, he paced and prayed. He kept reminding himself that he had to go by facts and not feelings. As a doctor, he was predisposed to believe in science, but something didn't feel right.

The beach at 4am was chaos. He tried to figure out who was in charge, but there seemed to be no order, not that he could discern. He began showing the picture desperately to anyone who would pause long enough to look at it. A young man approached him and told him that he needed to go; if he hadn't bought passage, he was slowing down the process. Ahmed tried to explain that he was only searching for his family, but the young man shoved him away.

Still, Ahmed persisted. Without his family, he was a man with nothing to lose. The young man came back to him, this time tapping Ahmed on the shoulder. When Ahmed turned, he was met with a punch to the face. An all-out brawl ensued, but Ahmed was outnumbered. The young man who was clearly part of the smuggling crew had been joined by a few others. Ahmed curled into a fetal position to absorb the blows.

In the distance, he heard a voice call out, "Enough!"

Ahmed stayed curled up until the same voice was now directly above him. "You alright?"

He coughed as he moved to a kneeling position, and the man held out his hand to help him to his feet.

"What seems to be the trouble?" the man asked, while the youngsters glared at him.

Ahmed wiped the blood from his lip. "I am looking for my family."

The man nodded, and then yelled at everyone to get back to work. "Are they on the beach now?" he said as he gestured to those climbing into the already-overcrowded boats.

"No." Ahmed fumbled to reach for the photo, his arm aching from one particularly well-placed kick. He showed it to the man who stood impassive.

"Haven't seen em. We don't keep lists of who crosses. You pay and you get a spot. Pay some extra we even throw in a life vest," he added with a small chuckle.

"Please allow me to show the photo. I mean no trouble."

"As you know, what we are doing here is illegal, so there can be no fuss. That is the only reason I stopped those three from beating you. You can go out and show the photo once more to those already boarded, but then you must leave. I am running a business here."

Ahmed nodded and headed to the water's edge. He waded into the sea and his shoes began to fill with sand. Using the flashlight on his phone, he showed the photo to each person who silently sat in the tiny boats. Each shook their head. Ahmed went as fast as he dared. The third boat was already pushing off when he was still making his trip around it. He was now chest deep, but no one had seen Safia or the children.

He staggered up the beach, his wet clothes and aching body slowing the process. He nodded at the "businessman," and made his way back to the hotel. He was a sight to see, walking back inside, dripping wet and bleeding. The young man who was manning the door asked what had happened. Ahmed just said that he'd tripped on the beach.

He tidied himself up and tried to get some sleep. The adrenaline had worn down by now and he was beginning to feel every blow he had received. He eventually managed to pass out for a few hours.

He was no closer to finding his family than when he'd started. The next morning, he returned to the police station to leave his contact information with the kindly sergeant, as well as the photo. He assured the man he had more.

"What happened?" the sergeant asked as he gestured toward Ahmed's very swollen black eye.

Ahmed simply shook his head, and went to leave. The sergeant, though, was not sure he had even seen a human being so broken before—and he had seen some horrible things in his twenty-seven years. He tried to bite his tongue, but then said the words he had been debating saying the day before.

"A few days back, two boats sunk. Most of those on board drowned. The Greek navy picked up the rest. If your family was on them, I cannot say, but I thought you should know."

Ahmed heard what the man was telling him but his brain couldn't quite process it. He may have said thank you before he left. He moved through the world in a fog, back to the hotel, and then to the airport.

His fog disappeared instantly when his phone rang. Caller Unknown flashed across the screen.

"Safia!!" he answered excitedly.

"Dr. Ahmed Bahar?" The young woman's voice. Her accent was clearly Syrian.

"Yes?"

"My name is Miss Samaan. I am with the embassy in London. I am calling to let you know the passports are ready, complete with the visas. You can pick them up at your earliest convenience."

THE RETURN
TO PARIS

1959

Eli was looking for the address of the Paris apartment, when he came across a letter addressed to his mother. It was from while they were in Cyprus. His French was more rusty than he expected, but he managed to read it aloud, though stumbling over certain words.

> *Hannah,*
>
> *I received your last letter, I am sorry to hear that you and Elijah were blocked entry to Palestine. I have also received no news on David. I am aware it is your sincere hope that he too is making his way to Palestine, but the offer stands for you and Eli to stay with me until he is located or for as long as you should want to. I know you will never love me the way you love David and that I can live with, but the thought of*

danger befalling you or Eli is something that I cannot live with. I have to remind myself that Celeste was never real, though she will always feel like my soulmate. I am being told the British will repatriate those on Cyprus to their home countries. If that is true, please return to me. Should you not want to return to France, please let me know when you and Eli are settled in Palestine so I may assist you in any way I can. I owe it you and I owe it to David. I will never forgive myself for what I didn't do.

    Louis

Eli racked his brain trying to remember a man named Louis, but that name meant nothing to him. His mother had never mentioned it. The name Celeste, however, rang a bell, but he didn't know why. The false papers his mother had purchased to cross into Vichy-controlled France had the names Sophie and Alexander, not Celeste. The letter was postmarked from Paris, so Eli figured that was a good place to start.

Eli felt like a stranger in the city of his birth, and the idea that he'd find something familiar was naive at best. Eli had felt lost in Israel and felt equally lost in Paris. The address he had was more than a decade old, and there was no telling what or who he would find. It seemed as if, directly after the war, the entire population of Europe was moving. He could not make out the last name on the envelope, and so, here he was, standing outside the house as the rain pounded down, searching for a man simply named Louis. It was possible—and likely—he didn't want to be found. The letter didn't tell the entire story but, clearly Louis had some regrets of his role during the war. Eli silently cursed himself for his folly.

A middle-aged woman from the apartment above called down, asking if she could be of assistance. Eli tried to look up, but the rain stung his eyes. The rain in Paris smelled like petrol and garbage, nothing like the sweet, earthy rain of the kibbutz. Eli explained he was looking for Louis, conveniently leaving out the last name. The woman explained he hadn't lived there since the occupation. Eli thanked her and turned to leave, but the woman added in that the woman next door had a forwarding address. She also remarked that she didn't know why he would keep an apartment he hadn't used for a decade.

He knocked on the door but no one answered. He was soaking wet and starving, so he abandoned his quest for that night. He found a sleazy hotel in a rundown building, but once inside, he couldn't rest. He looked through each of the letters and photos again, all but the letter from the Red Cross, that is. He knew what that one said; he didn't need to read it. He held on to the photo of what he could only guess was his first birthday, his parents on both sides of him smiling widely. He marveled at how young his mother looked.

In the morning, he strolled through the Marais. He knew he had lived there and it all looked familiar, but nothing stood out to him, no place that he could definitively say was his home. Returning to Louis' apartment, he once again tried the neighbor. At the door, an old woman eyed him suspiciously, demanding to know why he was looking for Mr. Dufort. Eli explained that he had been a friend of his parents Hannah and David Bronstein. The woman insisted she knew no such people and was ready to close the door when Eli added they were also friends of Celeste.

"Ahh, Celeste, what a sweet woman. Such a shame... A real beauty too," the woman sad sadly.

She invited Eli in while she wrote down Louis's address for him. He was hesitant to ask too any questions as he still didn't understand who Celeste was. He needed to tread carefully.

"The woman upstairs says he hasn't been back since the occupation?"

She nodded as she rifled through a desk. "Those were bad times for us all," she said. She then let out a little shriek of delight when she found what she was in search of.

"And Celeste?"

The woman gave Eli a puzzled look. "They found her washed up in the Seine. Louis was devastated. He left the city and never returned."

Eli was not sure if he wanted to know any more, but he had come this far, so he boarded the train to Calais. As the countryside flashed by, he thought of the other train trip he had taken from Paris to Marseille as a child. He remembered how lost he had felt. He thought this trip back to France would have answered some of his lingering questions, but it had only given him more.

From Calais, Eli began the walk to Sangette. He couldn't quite see the sea, but he could smell it in the air. A man driving past offered him a lift into town, which he gladly accepted. The two men made small talk. Eli asked him if he knew Louis Dufort. Surprisingly, the man, Remy, said that he did, and that he would drop Eli off at his cottage. Any ideas Eli may have had of turning back at the last moment were taken away from him, and for the rest of the way, they rode in silence.

The man was curious to what had brought Eli here, but he said nothing, and when they reached the cottage, he hopped out the truck. Eli gingerly knocked on the door, which only caused the driver to laugh and pound on the door himself. When no one answered, he called out, "Louis? Louis...are you home?"

A voice called out from the back yard. "Remy, is that you? I saw your truck. Give me a moment. I am almost done."

"There is a young man looking for you."

"What have I done now?" he called back, laughing as

he made his way to the front yard. When he appeared, he was wiping dirt from his hands with a rag.

He froze dead in his tracks when he saw Eli, the color drained from his skin. Louis stood there as if he had seen a ghost.

"I am—" Eli began, but Louis cut him off.

"Elijah!" The man outstretched his arms and pulled Eli toward him, weeping. "I thought you were your father." Indeed, Eli had grown up to look similar to his father, though his eyes were his mothers. His sandy blond hair had turned a chestnut color, and he still carried the awkward lengthiness of youth. He was on the shorter side, but Louis knew that he was David's. Louis wiped his eyes with the same rag he had wiped the dirt on, but it did little to stem the flow.

Remy had conveniently disappeared by the time Louis had regained his composure. Louis invited Eli inside and made himself busy putting food in front of him.

There were so many questions that neither man was quite sure where to begin. Eli pulled the letter from his bag and placed it on the table.

Louis touched it gingerly, as if the intimate, crinkled paper was a living, breathing thing. Wiping his eyes, he sat down slowly at the table.

"I am sure you have many questions," Louis said, choking on his words a little.

Eli sat motionless, not sure what to ask first. As he rolled the options through his head, the one that pushed its way to the front was, "Who was my mother to you?"

"Celeste. She was the love of my life."

"My mother's name was Hannah," he interjected.

Louis looked really distraught all of a sudden, and stood up to leave the table. "I owe you the entire story, and so much more, but this is a great shock to a man my age. Please stay for as long as you like, and you have my word you will have the truth, but not tonight."

Eli nodded, unsure what to do.

"Please make yourself at home, go down to the beach —it isn't too windy today." With that, Louis excused himself for the remainder of the night and for much of the next day. Eli went down to the beach, as suggested, borrowing one of the countless books Louis had stacked near the fireplace. He struggled to read the French, but pushed through a story regardless. The story was about a fisherman. When he tired of that, he wandered around the quaint village. Eli's presence in the sleepy hamlet was a novelty, which caused some excitement, but there was nothing that interesting to see, so he headed back to Louis' cottage. In the guest bedroom, he found his backpack had appeared, along with fresh linen. In the corner, sat another pile of books next to an abandoned trumpet.

The next morning, while holding a cup of tea and watching the waves , Eli was startled to see Louis appear next to him.

"Have you ever loved a woman?"

Thinking of Chaya, Eli didn't say anything.

"I can tell by your face you have. Are you running from her?"

"She married my best friend."

Louis smirked. "So, you will understand. Sit, and I will tell you a love story."

They sat on the beach and Louis wondered where to begin. With Eli being here, the story now spanned five decades.

"Your father and I grew up together, almost like brothers. Your grandmother worked for my mother. I suppose you could have said your grandmother was a maid, but it wasn't like that. My mother always said that Sarah, your grandmother, was her twin. My grandfather was a Baron in Switzerland, and my grandmother, as the story goes, was the most beautiful of women in all of Paris. My mother, Sophia was born out of wedlock and it was all quite scandalous, but shortly after she was born, my grandmother died. Some say it was during childbirth; some say the days following. The Baron, while he couldn't pass on the title, adored Sophia and provided the life that would befit the daughter of nobility. She was educated at the finest schools, and was given a lovely home in Paris. Your grandmother came to work in her household around the age of fifteen. And true enough, the women's lives, though incredibly different, did mirror one another. Both women married, had sons and then lost their husbands to the Great War. They became one another's strength.

"My mother was at Sarah's bedside the day she died. And your father with me when my mother passed.

"As the two women were lifelong companions, your father and I were inseparable from the day we were born right up until the war. Of course, we went to different schools and eventually found ourselves in different social circles, but we had a bond that couldn't be broken. He was a great piano player, and I played the trumpet. What a racket we caused. Oh, the stories of our mischief were legendary."

It was then that Eli, for the first time, remembered the piano in the apartment. He could almost see his father fiddling on the keys.

"Did you know, before he became a bookbinder, he wanted to be a composer?"

Eli shook his head. He had never heard this story. There were so many stories he didn't know.

"But when he met your mother, all that changed. Till this day, she is still the most beautiful woman I have ever seen in real life. Beyond that, she was smart, and sweet and loved a practical joke. He wanted more than anything to marry her, so he found a job as an intern as a book binder. Sure, he would still play and compose in his free time, but they were happy. And then you were born. Such a fat baby! I, on the other hand, considered myself a playboy. The considerable wealth left to my mother was now mine and I was going to have as much fun as I could. I didn't have a care in the world."

Louis took a deep breath before continuing. "And then the war changed everything. One day, your mother showed up at my door looking like death. She explained that she had taken you to try to cross into the free zone, but saw a woman and child killed right in front of her. She had left you with nuns—it was her only option as she had no papers and no money. She returned to Paris, but she had found out your father had been taken by the Vel' D'hiv' Roundup. She was in such a state. It pains me to even think of it now. She had walked most of the way trying to make it back to your father. In weeks, she had lost everything: her home, her husband, her child…"

Eli said nothing.

"She asked only to stay the night. I was the only one in Paris she trusted. Then she intended to try to find your father. It was both an act of love and desperation —and a suicide mission. I was only able to convince her to stay till we sorted out new papers for her. I was still working as a musician then. The Nazis loved jazz 'cause they thought it hedonistic. I was still working at some of the fancier hotels, when a member of the resistance approached me. He said that all I had to do was listen, that if I heard anything interesting I was to report back. It was through this new contact I was able to get your mother new papers in the name of Celeste Barbier."

"So that's what you meant in your letter, when you said she didn't exist. So, who did they find in the Seine?"

"Please, you must understand the entire story." Louis exhaled. "While this was happening, we had been able to piece together that you father was first sent to Drancy, and then to Auschwitz. There were rumors, of course, but even then we thought they were just labor camps. We both believed your father was strong and we hoped the end of the war would come soon. Even your mother knew she couldn't make it to him, so for that time, she became Celeste. We told everyone she was my fiancée, and she would often join me on nights when I played in the hotels."

"Play for the Nazis, you mean?" Eli asked, his tone repugnant.

"Yes, for the Nazis. I am not proud of it, but we all did what we had to in order to survive. One night in late 42—or early 43, I only remember it was winter—when we were leaving the hotel, a woman recognized your mother. She began screaming the most hateful things. She screamed things that I won't even repeat, but all because your mother was a Jew. It caused quite a commotion in the street and we ran in fear. At one of bridges, we stopped and we tossed her shoes, handbag and her overcoat. I took her to the train station early the next morning, and sent her here."

"She was here?"

"For the remainder of the war. I left three days later, telling anyone who would listen that my beautiful fiancée had thrown herself into the Seine. Eventfully they found her coat and what not. I first headed to Reims in case I was being watched, but I arrived finally in Sangette, relieved to see your mother was here, staring at the sea through the kitchen window. Of course, the beach looked very different then—the Germans had bunkers and heavy artillery lined up across it. I had sent her to an honest nest, but there was nowhere safe. It was here that I fell in love with her, as we lived in plain sight of the Germans. They were all over the village, but your mother never dropped her guard. She knew that her survival—and seeing you again—depended on this act."

"And did she love you?"

"When Calais fell, we hid for days in the cellar while the beach was bloodied. We knew it was a matter of weeks, days even, till the war was over. But in the year spent in this house, I had fallen hopelessly in love with your mother. I believed the act. I believed that when we danced in the kitchen she also felt what I felt, or when she mended my sweater, she did so out of love for me. I confessed my love to her, expecting to hear the same, but she only ever loved your father."

"And then what?"

"Paris was liberated. Calais was liberated. She told me she would always love me but, her heart could never belong to anyone but David. I told her I could still love her and you. I begged her not to go, or let me go with her. If nothing else, I asked that she would come back if she could not locate David. I only ever heard from her once more. She sent me a letter from Cyprus. She said she suspected the worst, but still would not let herself believe David was dead." He stopped for a moment and then gave a chuckle. "She also said you had become so tall..."

Eli filled in the rest of the story: the woman Louis loved, regardless of her name, had died in an internment camp in Cyprus.

"Did you ever marry?" Eli asked.

"No, my heart always belonged to you mother. And because I loved her, I hoped she had found your father. I tried for a while to find you both, but I had no luck. If I had known she died, I would have come for you."

"And why have you not been back to Paris?"

Staring out at the sea Louis replied, "Too many ghosts."

THE CROSSING

2015

The blackened sea could be heard but barely seen. Safia tried to let her eyes adjust to the darkness. There was no moon, or if there was, it had placed itself behind clouds. Just as well, Safia thought. The crossing was illegal. She was preparing to do what she'd told herself—and what she had promised Ahmed—she would never do.

"One week," Safia had chanted to herself after her last call with Ahmed. One week till passports, one week till they could leave. She hated herself for the way she had spoken to him. She didn't blame him. She'd called and apologized, but she knew she couldn't undo her words. But in the last week so much had transpired —things she couldn't explain, but as a mother she *sensed* it.

It began the same day as that call to Ahmed. On the way back from the beach, they had stopped for ice cream. Safia had seen a man staring at her, and when she looked back to catch his gaze, she could have sworn it was Emir. She had quickly gathered up Asma and Nadir, and hurried back to the safehouse, making sure that she hadn't been followed. That night, she didn't sleep at all, and every siren in the distance made her blood turn to ice. By the next morning, in the peaceful home of Rabia and Ibrahim, she had begun to shake the feeling. But when she went back to the beach, she saw him again—this time she was sure of it.

With the comings and goings of the house, Safia couldn't rest. New people would appear one day only to be gone the next. She knew that this was the real purpose of the house, but Rabia assured her she was welcome for as long as she needed. It felt as if she was always waiting for the rug to be pulled out from under her. She had been lost in her thoughts when her phone rang. Without looking, she answered it.

"Ahmed?" she asked, perplexed as to why he would be phoning at this moment, as they had set times they would call each other. It was the best way to relieve the constant worry for them both. But Ahmed wasn't there; just a constant rhythmic clicking noise. She hung up and looked at the screen, thinking they had had bad connection, but it wasn't Ahmed. She hadn't given anyone else the number.

The calls kept coming. Always the same clicking noise. Safia stopped answering, leaving the calls to feed through to her voicemail. Her inbox became full of those noises: click...click...click.

Day blended into night and back into day. Still, Safia chanted to herself: "one week." And so it began, this constant ebb and flow of intense panic, always accompanied by her reassurances to herself that she was imagining it all.

A week passed and there were no passports. This time, Ahmed was told it would only be "three more days." Safia could barely hear him when he told her this as her heart was beating in her ear so loudly. She couldn't remember the last time she'd slept. That morning, Rabia had said the pharmacist had questioned her about the insulin. Rabia had shrugged it off, but Safia remembered how Emir had handed her a vial when he made his threat. It all made sense to her now: spotting Emir on the beach, the spam calls, the questions about Nadir's insulin.

But the moment that changed everything was that night when the police showed up. She watched the strobe lights from their car dance across the ceiling. She didn't dare look out the window, but held Nadir and Asma close and urged them to be silent. It sounded like the commotion was at the next house over, but she couldn't be sure. She waited for the knock to come, but it didn't. Still, she sat there, paralyzed in fear, until right before sunrise.

She dressed the children in an automated, robotic fashion, securing the small bags that each carried on their backs, and snuck from the house. Staying with Rabia and Ibrahim, she had learned where to go to meet with a smuggler and knew what to expect when arriving in Greece. The camps on the islands were horrible and overcrowded, but they were in the EU and that was all that mattered. And Greece would be more than happy to let any Syrian with a visa pass on anywhere else.

Safia stopped at an ATM and took as much money as it would allow. The passage, despite its danger, was very expensive. Rabia did everything she could to talk Safia out of it, but had eventually said that she understood if she had to go, even if it was for reasons Rabia didn't understand. But she made her promise one thing: that they would have life jackets. That was one promise Safia intended to keep.

They had stayed at the smugglers all day, feeling uneasy. Nervous tension filled the room. Of course, the passage itself would be dangerous, but even getting out to sea could be a problem. Turkey was supposedly patrolling the beaches to make sure no one was even attempting the crossing. In all her trips to the beach, Safia had never seen any patrols, but still this rumor hung in the air like a toxic gas. Scanning the room, Safia wondered how the others had found themselves here. Did they have visas waiting for them on the other side or was their desperation so great that it didn't matter?

Safia watched a young couple with a chubby infant.

They reminded her of herself and Ahmed when they were first married, when they'd only had Nadir and Asma. The man noticed her gaze and introduced himself as Saad, and then his wife, Fatima, and their baby, Rima. Asma was enchanted with the baby immediately. She had stunning charcoal eyes that sparkled. They made small talk as they waited for the sun to set. Saad said he had been a school teacher in Homs before the war, his wife Fatima a secretary. He made Asma and Nadir giggle, and Safia thought that he must have been a wonderful teacher. Saad said he had a cousin in Scotland and that was where they hoped to settle as a family. Safia wondered if they would make it, with the borders being closed, and movement restricted. Without visas, most would get stuck in Greece, but once she was in the EU, she knew she would be safe. From there, she'd only need to meet up with Ahmed.

That evening when they spoke, she apologized for missing his call earlier in the day, but she told him that she loved him and that she knew he was doing everything he could to get the family to safety. She did not tell him what she was about to do. She would beg for forgiveness once they were together. He would understand then. She told him she would call in the morning.

As the sunset came and night began to set in, Fatima told Safia that she was scared. Safia tried to reassure her that it would be fine, but as midnight approached, she too could feel her nerves giving way. Fatima hoped this was finally the new start that they had all hoped for.

The plan was to leave in the middle of the night, so as the sun rose, they would likely already be in Greek waters, eventually getting picked up by the coast guard and taken ashore. Getting picked up by the Turkish coast guard would have a very different outcome, one that Safia wouldn't let herself think about.

The boat was more than a little dingy, yet Safia counted roughly forty people crammed on, then another fifteen at the last moment and all but pushed out to sea. She had fastened the life vests around Asma and Nadir and herself. She had paid a small fortune for them and prayed she wouldn't need them. Saad and Fatima, nor the baby had life vests, nor did half the people. A man on the beach, who seemed to be slightly in charge, explained that it was about "ten to fifteen kilometers to Lesbos." Then he added, "When the sun is up you can see it."

The motor attached the boat was not powerful and progress was slow. Safia couldn't tell if the water was choppy or if it was simply that the tiny boat was overloaded. An hour passed and then another as the sea turned darker. The only noise was the tiny motor which continued to strain under the pressure. No one said a word. Sometimes a cough could be heard or a whimper from one of the babies. Safia nodded off, but was awakened by the sound of the waves and the impact as they crashed against the sides of the boat.

Opening her eyes, she could see that they were now in open water. Panic started to fill the air as the waves continued to grow. Safia tried to calm Asma and Nadir but every new wave reignited their panic.

She retied their backpacks around them—another tip from Rabia—and retightened their life jackets, assuring the children that the boat wasn't sinking. But it was. The blackness of night had begun to fade and Safia could see the waves.

Shrieks filled the air as the cold water began to pool around them. The smuggler had already flung himself into the water, And Safia caught sight of Fatima silently sobbing as they too slid into the water. As they went under, Safia momentarily lost sight of Nadir.

"Nadir!" she called into the chaos, fighting to be heard above the other people who were also shouting their loved one's names. She felt an intense pain radiate from her back, but in her terror for Nadir, she barely registered it.

She heard his muffled scream and saw a young man holding onto him in a panic, trying to stay afloat. The man was drowning Nadir. She screamed, but to no avail. She was too far away. She tried to swim, but the waves were too powerful and it took all her strength to hold on to Asma. She inched closer, but she was too slow. Thankfully, Saad was much closer, and began to punch the man repeatedly until he relented, but he was too late: Nadir no longer needed his life jacket.

The panic was starting to subside as those with life jackets bobbed in the water and those without gave into the pull of the sea. Safia stroked Nadir's face and kissed him, before slipping his life jacket over his head. She handed it to Saad, who then took Rima from Fatima's arms so she could do what she could to fasten it around herself. The baby was sputtering and choking; how Fatima had managed to tread water with the infant in her arms would be known only to God himself.

Safia began to removed her own life vest, but tried to stop her. She reached around to her back and when she pulled her hand away, she saw it was covered in blood. She knew she had hit something sharp when she went into the water, most likely the propeller. Either way, she was losing a lot of blood and she had to fight to stay conscious.

At the sight of the blood, Saad understood immediately, and took the life jacket from her. "Please look after Asma," she said to him. "Her father is in London."

Safia could barely stay above water as she was still holding Nadir, but in that last moment, she managed to tell Asma, "Don't worry, the boats will be here soon. Saad and Fatima will help you get to Daddy. I love you, my princess." She kissed the top of Asma's head, before finally giving in to the water.

ISRAEL

1962-1967

Eli stayed with Louis for three months. Louis was able to fill in so many gaps in Eli's past, as well as showing him photos of Louis and David as children. It was as if Louis was finally able to provide him with real memories aside from the fractured ones within his own mind.

Still, Eli was torn. France was not home, nor did he have one in Israel. It was as if he was always adrift at sea. He told Louis the story of Chaya and Ben, the proposal, the wedding. Louis nodded through it all, and Eli kept waiting for the old man to give an opinion on the situation, but he didn't. It didn't come up again until the night before Eli was to leave. As the sun was setting, the men sat at the patio set drinking beers, when Louis finally commented.

"Don't let them go."

"What?" Eli replied not following.

"Chaya and Ben. Don't let them go. They are your family. And Lord knows we could all use some more of that."

"But she chose him."

"But you can still love them, and still do. Don't make the same mistakes as me. I would have rather had you, you mother and your father in my life, even if she choose him every second of every day. Don't let your pride stop you from having a full life."

Eli resisted the urge to tell the old man that he simply didn't understand, because he could tell he did, though he couldn't always fully reconcile himself with this idea.

As they were saying their goodbyes, Eli had one more question for Louis: the address of his family apartment. Eli couldn't explain it, but he wanted to see it. Louis nodded and wrote it down. As Eli reached for the piece of paper, Louis held on to it for a moment and said, "You won't find what you are looking for there. Go home, build a life. And don't forget to write."

***

Eli stood for a long time outside the building. He had no memories of this place, despite his best attempts to conjure them. He stood there longer than he intended, thinking that he would feel something, but Louis was right; whatever it was he was looking for was not here. Still, he couldn't tear himself away. He found the exact apartment on the second floor. The window box was filled was pink flowers. Did his mother have window boxes? He made it to the door but couldn't bring himself to knock. The tragedy was enough for one family. What was he hoping to find twenty years later? Yet, when he left, he still had that nagging feeling that he had indeed left behind a piece of the puzzle.

Back in Israel, Eli settled in Jerusalem. Eli wasn't sure what he wanted to do, but he knew the kibbutz life was not for him, so instead he registered for math and science classes at Hebrew University, after some persuasion from Louis and the offer to help with tuition. Once he was registered, Louis, true to his word, sent money every month to help cover expenses. But Eli sent it back, only for the following month to be sent double the amount. Though he felt guilty for accepting it, the job he had at the bakery did little to cover his lodging and tuition. Eli promised that he would pay Louis back, no matter how long it took.

Eli also reached out to Chaya and Ben, and though awkward at first, it almost felt like old times when the three of them were together. It was a rare occasion that everyone was able to be in the same place at the same time, but when all three were laughing and telling stories that became grander each time they were told, everything felt as it should. Ben was still busy trying to climb the military ladder, and each promotion and new rank meant less time at home. Chaya and Eli were each were lonely in their own ways. They wrote to each other, as calls were still quite expensive—. Chaya's only desire was still to become a mother, but she was having trouble conceiving. Still, she worked in the children's home on the kibbutz and that was something. Eli assured her that her turn would come, though he knew nothing on the matter at all. Chaya would go through "bad spells," according to Ben, though he did what he could. But it was like the weather: there was no predicting it.

Eli found himself enrolled in medical school, a path he would have never guessed for himself, and he eventually switched from general medicine and decided to become an ophthalmologist, after accidentally stumbling into a lecture on disease of the eyes that piqued his curiosity.

In 1965, Eli graduated with honors. There to watch him do so was Ben, Chaya and Louis, who had flown in from France. Eli couldn't see it from the stage, but Chaya later told him that Louis was wiping tears from his eyes as he watched him get handed his diploma. In the five years, Louis had aged considerably and was nearly frail. The once-spritely man could now only shuffle, supported by a cane. His rapid decline surprised Eli, but Louis would not let the conversation turn to him. There was only one reason for the occasion, he said, and that was to celebrate Eli's success. Chaya and Ben teased him, saying that now that he was Dr. Elijah Bronstein, he needed a wife. Eli laughed it off, but Chaya could tell that the joke stung and quickly changed the subject.

Ben and Chaya had moved to Tel Aviv when his job at the Department of Defense looked to be more permanent. Though happy to be moving up the ladder, Ben often dreaded the desk work, but the move to Tel Aviv had been good for them both. Chaya hadn't had any of her "spells" since living in the city, and whenever she felt one coming, she would simply talk to the sea and that seemed to do the trick. She had found a job as a kindergarten teacher in a private school and was the happiest she could ever remember being. They were still trying for children and had seen several specialists in the city, but all just confirmed that there seemed to be something wrong without any idea what exactly that was or how to fix it. Ben was not open to the idea of adoption, but told Chaya if—in a few more years of trying they still couldn't conceive —he would reconsider.

But none of that was on Chaya's mind when Eli came. He had three weeks before starting his new permanent position at Hadassah Hospital, and so had promised to visit.

Tel Aviv was a different world than Jerusalem. Jerusalem was a divided city, still cut down the middle with a wall. Jordan controlled the eastern part of the city and the potential for violence was ever present. Louis had remarked that he was not sure why Eli would want to live in such a place, and Eli merely quipped that he was used to living behind walls, a joke that Louis didn't find funny. Either way, Eli liked the city. It was like a world unto itself, combining the modern and the old. Though not a deeply religious man, and for reasons Eli couldn't articulate, Jerusalem simply felt right to him. It gave him what he thought he would have felt at the apartment in Paris: a sense of history and home. Tel Aviv, on the other hand, was firmly planted in the future—and not Eli's—in the way it moved full speed ahead toward modernity.

Chaya had tried to convince Eli to move to Tel Aviv, but Eli knew that he could only stand so much temptation—he was only human. He had to keep reminding himself that Chaya was married to Ben. He couldn't help but wonder how different life would have been if he had asked her first.

Eli returned to Jerusalem and life went on as normal until 1967. There had always been whispers of war in the air, but even this time felt different to Eli. Ben couldn't tell his oldest friend that he thought war was coming, but the writing was on the wall. Eli had hoped for peace, but when all the army reserves were called up for duty, he knew that a peaceful resolution was no longer an option.

When Israel went to war that summer, both Eli and Ben went with her. Ben, by this time was a commander, and both were sent to the Golan Heights, which remained peaceful for the first few days of the war. It was only the calm before the storm. On June 5th, Israel began its assault, decimating Syrian airfields. The battle waged on, with Israeli forces moving further and further into Syrian-controlled territory. Eli's tank unit was stationed in a defense position to protect civilian settlements that had been bombarded previously, while Ben, on the other hand, was at the front, pushing troops forward and engaging in hand-to-hand combat. Israel was able to capture key strongholds, but not without cost. When the ceasefire came only five days later on June 10th, there was euphoria in the streets. Jerusalem has been reunited. The Golan Heights, West Bank and the Sinai had been captured. It was a resounding victory.

The celebrations were short-lived for Eli, though, when word came that a commander had been killed. He shook the thought from his mind—there was more than one commander in the army, after all—but the worst was eventually confirmed. During the battle, Ben, who had always led from the front, had been caught by a Syrian sniper bullet. His men said he was still giving orders as he bled out. While those around Eli were jovial—and had every right to be—Eli sunk down to the floor and wept. He couldn't really remember crying for his dad, or even his mother—he remembered being scared when she had died, but this grief was more than Eli could bear. As much as he had hated Ben for winning Chaya, he knew that it was never real hate, and at that moment he could only mourn. Chaya had chosen Ben, not only because he had asked first, but because there was something in Ben's very nature that made people feel protected. Even Eli had felt safer in the world knowing that Ben was there.

Death and war go hand and hand—both men had known this was a remote possibility that one of them might not return, and Eli had promised Ben that should that fate should come to be, he would be the one to tell Chaya. It was a promise made over beers around a bonfire on the kibbutz, the type that you make, but never give another thought to. Eli never really expected to carry out this wish. Ben had been the strongest and most confident person he had ever known. People like that simply don't die. As children, Ben's self-assuredness made him a practical joker, and even now, Eli just wanted to believe this was a horrible joke. But he was not a child anymore; he knew better. There was no time in his life that Eli could remember his heart feeling so black and hollow at the same time. It was too much to bear. A world without Ben didn't make sense.

Eli's thoughts turned toward Chaya, and for a moment, he hated Ben again. How could he do this to her?

Eli tried to figure out what he would say when he saw her. There were no good words. But though he had rehearsed what he was going to say over and over, in the end, he didn't need to say a word. When Chaya opened the door and saw Eli, his bloodshot eyes and broken-hearted smile, she knew. Eli stayed with her while she wept. At the funeral, he didn't know what to do. The pain he saw on Chaya's face made him wish it would have been him instead of Ben.

Eli didn't want to leave Chaya alone, but his life was back in Jerusalem. Ben's parents were still on the kibbutz, but she didn't want to return there. He managed to convince her to come stay with him for a few weeks. Chaya was like a ghost, there but absent, so she didn't put up too much of fight when he all but insisted. It unnerved him that she had become so silent. She had wept at the news and at the funeral. Eli at least knew how to respond to tears.

He gave Chaya his bed and spent the night on the couch, staring at the ceiling. He couldn't sleep. He could tell that Chaya was awake as well.

He softly knocked on the door jam. She looked at him.

"Can't sleep either?" he asked.

"No. What time is it?"

"It's almost 4am. Would you like to go for a walk?"

"Alright. Let me get dressed."

As they meandered the streets of the Old City, Chaya ran her hand along the white stone. The walls still held the warmth of the sun, even though the night was cool. She asked excitedly if they could go to the wailing wall. Eli hesitated. Though the Old City had been recaptured, there were still land mines along the road, and still now, every few days a sniper would be found, still unwilling to give up. Yet, the excitement in Chaya's voice made him surrender his common sense.

Earlier that day, thousands had streamed into the Old City, crossing from Mount Zion, to celebrate the Jewish holiday of Shavuot at the Western Wall, so it had to be relatively safe. And so they weaved through the Old City, the stones under foot slippery from centuries of use. Most of it was empty. A few soldiers stopped them to ask their purpose, but let them continue on.

Finally, they reached the street—really more of an alley—where the wailing wall stood. Across the way, the neighborhood that had been there had been evacuated and the buildings would eventually be demolished to make way for a plaza. There were two others at the wall praying. Chaya could hear their lips moving but not the words. She gingerly touched the wall, and began to pray. Eli, who was not a religious man, stood back and watched her. If she had prayed before this, Eli had never seen it. He thought he saw a tear roll down her cheek but he let her be. She stood there a long time. The summer sun began to rise but he was content to simply stay with her for as long as she needed.

She didn't say much when she was done. It wasn't until they had breakfast in a tiny cafe that she finally broke her silence: "My father, though I remember very little of him, promised one day we would pray at the wall. He was a very devout and learned man, and he knew one day it would be true. It was the only promise he made to me that has come true. I know it is crazy but I wanted to touch it, to know its real, not simply an idea or a hope. To know some promises are true, ya know?"

Eli nodded, but he didn't quite grasp what she was talking about. It occurred to him that there was really so much about her that he still didn't know. Though they had grown up together, he knew so little of the woman she had become, and even less about her past. It was the first time Eli had ever even heard her mention one of her parents.

Chaya was talking, remarking about the coffee or the jam or something equally as inconsequential, when Eli's attention became diverted. It was because of a man with his grey hair slicked back, smoking a cigarette with long slow drags. Eli had to adjust his eyes a few times. Chaya looked over her shoulder to see what Eli was starting at so intently.

The man rose to greet a woman, whose face Eli couldn't see. Still staring, Chaya asked who it was. Eli didn't hear her, as he was so fixated on the couple. When the man let out a laugh, Eli knew he had been right.

"Come with me!" he said, grabbing Chaya hand.

They approached the table slowly. The man caught Eli's gaze first.

"Eli!!" he said, wrapping both arms around him, and then pulled away to take another look.

"Yossi!" Eli said before hugging him again.

"Vera, you remember Eli," he said, turning to the woman next to him. "We met—"

Vera slapped him on the shoulder playfully. "Of course I remember Eli. And is that you, Chaya?"

Chaya nodded and hugs were exchanged between them. Chaya hadn't stayed in Cyprus long, but the entire time she had been practically glued to Vera's hip. For Vera, it had not been easy to say goodbye to any of the children, but Chaya was one she would often wonder about from time to time. The doll-like child seemed too fragile for this world.

"Please join us," Yossi insisted.

They exchanged their highlights from the last twenty years. Vera and Yossi acted like proud parents when they found out that Eli had become a doctor. They had been determined to stay in the camp in Cyprus until it closed, but Vera returned a few months after Chaya and Eli as she received the wonderful news that she was expecting. With word of war on the horizon, Yossi also returned to Israel and in 1948, he had fought to help secure the Negev. After the war, Yossi had become a bus driver for Egged. Vera had always wanted a large family—their five children made her home one of chaos but one of love.

"And you two, do you have children?" Vera asked.

Eli looked down and stammered, "We aren't married."

"Oh, I am sorry. I saw the wedding ring and assumed."

Chaya hadn't even thought about it, how it might look that she was still wearing her wedding band while in public with another man. She placed her hands under the table on her lap.

"I am widowed. He was in Syria," Chaya said, stifling a crack in her voice.

Vera nodded, immediately aware of her mistake, but unable to undo it. Yossi steered the conversation back to more pleasant—if not trivial—topics.

"Have you seen the Old City yet?" Yossi asked, speaking as if it was still a novelty.

"It so charming," Chaya said. The rest of the table gave her a surprised look. The Old City was nearly vacant, bullet riddled and lacking most comforts; charming was the last word most would have used.

Before they said their goodbyes, Vera was adamant that they should come to dinner. Eli attempted to politely decline, but Yossi gave him a mischievous grin that told him it was futile to resist. The two women were already exchanging details anyway.

When they arrived at their house, Vera kept apologizing for the state of the place. It was small house in Nachlaot. The white stone made it seem stately, although it wasn't. Chaya thought there was almost something romantic about it. Thinking back to her modern, yet empty, Tel Aviv apartment, she shuddered.

Eli thought that Chaya had never looked more beautiful. Yossi and Vera kept passing each other knowing grins as they ate the dinner Vera had prepared.

While Chaya and Vera did the dishes, Yossi invited Eli outside for a cigarette. Like at the cafe, Yossi took long slow drags.

"Savoring them," he explained.

Eli choked on his cigarette. He wasn't a smoker, but he knew that the other option was staying alone in the dining room with four of the five children, the oldest now enlisted.

"It's not wrong to want to be happy, you know," Yossi said as he stamped out his cigarette and turned to go back into the house.

"Excuse me?"

But Yossi kept on walking.

The following day, Eli woke up, ready to return to work at the hospital. Rumor had it that, for first time in almost twenty years, the hospital would once again be operating from Mount Scopus. This caused excitement amongst the doctors, but at the thought of returning to work, Eli felt a sense of dread. He would return to his routine, Chaya would return to Tel Aviv, and the past few weeks would become a memory. Yossi's words echoed in his head, until he could no longer lay still. He paced until he saw Chaya standing at the door.

"I am sorry. I didn't mean to wake you."

"You didn't. I couldn't sleep either. I don't want to be alone tonight." She reached out her hand to him, inviting him in, and he slid into the bed next to her and cradled her tightly.

When he needed to leave for work, he kissed her forehead and slipped out of bed. At work, he found out that the rumor was in fact true: the hospital would be reactivated on Mount Scopus. But Eli could have been informed that the hospital would be moving to the moon, for all he cared; his thoughts were elsewhere.

On the way home, he bought a bouquet of lilies for Chaya, but he returned home to find the apartment was empty. A wave of panic rushed over him, He frantically opened the dresser drawer that he had cleared when she first came, and breathed a sigh of relief when he saw her belongings were still there. He was clutching her clothes when she appeared.

"What are you doing?"

After one bound that moved him across the bedroom, he was holding her in his arms.

"Chaya, I thought you had gone. Please don't go. Stay with me. Marry me. I will live in Tel Aviv, or the bullet-riddled Old City that you find so charming, or a house by the sea, or anywhere you want. I have loved you since I was eleven. Please be my wife. I know this is the worst timing in the entire world, but when I thought you had gone, I knew my heart couldn't survive losing you twice."

Chaya returned to Tel Aviv the next morning. She packed the last of her things, made arrangements for the furniture and said goodbye to the sea. She then returned to the kibbutz for a time.

Chaya and Eli were married six months later. She was given away by Ben's parents.

GREECE

2015

Asma stood on the beach, the rocky shore was cold under her feet. She had lost her shoes in the ocean. Her little backpack, like everything else, was waterlogged, the change of clothes it held inside, completely soaked.

When the horn from a navy ship had sounded, Saad had raised his hand and shouted. Of the fifty-five people who had been in the dingy from Turkey, he could only count fifteen at most. But the joy had spread when it became apparent that it was the Greek coast guard. They were each plucked from the water and brought on board for the very short ride to Lesvos. When they disembarked, Saad had assumed Asma was right behind him, but when he looked around she had disappeared.

There was a flurry of activity around Asma. People were rushing ashore, some crying, some looking toward the heaven in thanks. Aid workers were helping unload boats, and then dismantling them. Life jackets were stacked in a large orange heap in the sand. Others scanned the horizon for more boats with binoculars. The boat had come just as her mother had promised, but she didn't see her mother or brother. She stood there, staring into the dark water. There was no one left on the boat. Was there another? So she sat down, and hugged her knees closely to her chest and waited. Her clothes were soaked, but she shivered from fear not cold. In the heavy activity, no one seemed to notice the small child peering into the ocean.

An aid worker finally noticed Asma and went to her, wrapping a thermal blanket around her shoulders. It would not be the first or last orphan to have ended up on the shore. If there was one universal truth it was that mothers, who only had one life jacket would always put in on the child.
"What is your name?" the kindly man asked in broken Arabic.

Asma didn't answer. She simply kept watch for the next boat. She couldn't see it, but it had to be there with her mother and Nadir. The man extended a hand to her but she sat still.

"Asma! Asma?" a woman cried out. Her calls mirrored others on the beach, who were also looking for relatives pulled from the sea.

Asma heard her name and turned to look for her

mother, but it wasn't her. It was Fatima. Fatima hugged her and the man, content that she had someone, left. Saad and Rima joined them moments later. Saad had to carry Asma off the beach as she was unwilling to leave without her mother.

The family was welcomed and given hot tea before being processed through the camp called Moria. Each person was photographed, fingerprinted and asked the location of their birth. When Saad claimed Asma as his own daughter, Fatima opened her mouth to interject but stopped herself. Both said nothing, as they were unsure what would happen to the child should it be discovered she was there alone. As they were Syrians, they were given three-month papers to stay in Greece.

It was not like the camps in Turkey. The fencing was high and topped with barb wire, and the sanitation was worse yet. The camp—nor, really, any of the islands—could handle the influx. In 2015, like Fatima, Saad, Asma and Rima, nearly four hundred thousand people would be pulled from the sea.

That night, Fatima sang both Asma and Rima a lullaby. She smoothed the little girl's hair back, doing what she could to settle her. The poor girl had seen her mother and brother be swallowed by the blackness of the Mediterranean. She still hadn't uttered a word.

Once Fatima thought Asma was asleep, Asma heard Fatima tell Saad, "We need to leave her here. We can hardly afford for us to travel onward."

"Nonsense." Saad smiled. "We promised her mother."

"That child has lost everything, and she hasn't said a single word. There are aid organizations here better suited to help her."

"We cannot leave her."

"Saad, please. She will only slow us down."

Without another word, Saad disappeared from the makeshift shelter. It was only a piece of tarp connected to the limbs of trees, and held up by a pole on the other side. It offered no protection from the wind, noise or smells. The children were huddled together on cardboard boxes. When Asma was sure Fatima was asleep, she pulled her tiny pink backpack toward her. From inside a sandwich bag, she pulled the postcard from her father out, and tucked it under her shirt so she could feel close to him. Then she cried herself to sleep.

The next day while Saad slept, Fatima set out to find food, taking Asma with her. What was available was rotten. The fruit had turned, the bread was either stale or molded. But Fatima picked off the worst of the mold and handed the rest to Asma. She brought the same moldy bread back to Saad and he ate the entire thing.

Within the squalor of the camp, there was nothing to occupy the time, so Saad left to inquire about passage to the mainland. They wanted to get "on the road," as quickly as possible—a term that referred to the coming path of refugees and migrants from Greece into Western Europe: first Greece to Macedonia and then to Serbia and onward; most hoped to end in Germany. Fatima did what she could to keep Asma comforted, but the child shook with fear.

"Can I look in your bag?" she asked her.

Asma only nodded.

There were some clothes, which were now beginning to turn moldy. Fatima laid them over the line which held up the tarp, but kept a sharp eye on them to make sure they didn't disappear. Asma had been provided a pair of shoes—though slightly too large—by one of the humanitarian groups on the beach. It was just as well, as there was not a second pair of shoes in the bag. There was a small tube of toothpaste and a toothbrush. Fatima tapped it to remove the sand before handing it back to Asma. She continued to look through the contents, hoping there was something that could lead to Asma's father. If there was a hint of a location, she could hand her over to Greek authorities. Instead, all she found was a small plastic bag which held a couple band aids, a pair of socks and 130 Turkish Lira.

Fatima placed it all back as it was, with the exception of the liras, all the while smiling at Asma. When the clothes were dry, Fatima gathered up Rima and Asma and set out once again for food, this time with money in hand. She was very frugal, only spending a third of it, and was able to find some good bread, an apple and a liter of water. The rest of the money she tucked away. When she returned to their tent, Saad scolded her for wandering off. Fatima apologized.

Asma had to use the bathroom, but the lines were so long that Fatima held up one Rima's baby blankets instead, while she squatted near a tree. Fatima worried how she would be able to keep Rima healthy in such a place. The conditions were appalling and there was nowhere to go; it was an island, after all. Everyone seemed to be waiting, but no one was sure what for.

They endured weeks of this until September, when, due to public outcry and the sheer overcrowding, Greece began to transport thousands of refugees to the mainland. It wasn't until months later that Fatima found out from a fellow refugee that this would be one of the last transports from Lesbos. Unknown to everyone, a deal would be made with Turkey the following year: refugees would either be detained in Moira indefinitely, or be sent back to Turkey.

As they boarded the boat headed to Athens, Asma was nervous. She didn't like the idea of going back to the sea, but Fatima held her hand tightly. When the boat docked, the crowds surged forward to get off. Asma looked, but she could see neither Saad or Fatima. She didn't know if she should stay where she was, as that was the instructions her parents had told her if she ever got separated, with the promise that they would come back and find her. Five minutes passed and there was no one. She began to panic.

When Saad looked down, he didn't see Asma. He called out and through the crowd that was surging forward to disembark, and thankfully, he saw her. He tugged on her arm, and Asma smiled as he reached out for her. When they were finally on land, Fatima exclaimed, "Oh, thank god. There you are!" and kissed the top of the girl's head.

The three-month pass for the EU was still good for a few weeks, and then at that time they would have to apply for asylum else be deported back to Syria. Saad did what he could to try to make it across Europe while their passes were still good. They even had to spend one night on the streets of Athens. Days were spent on trains or on foot, from one entry point to the next. Each train station looked the same to Asma, with the signs giving place names she couldn't pronounce—Gevgelija, Presevo, Tovarnik... There were hundreds on the roads and in every station. Asma wondered if everyone was going to the same spot. In Tovarnik, Fatima met a kind woman who said she had been there months as she had ran out of money to go any further. Fatima quietly asked the woman if there was a society for orphans nearby. The woman looked at the two sleeping children and then back at Fatima, alarmed. She told her there was nothing in the city she knew of.

It was in Gevgelija, beyond the confines of a traditional camp or detention center, that Saad reached the end of his tether, and violently rifled through Asma's bag. He was insistent that there had to be something that said who she belonged to or at least some money. Fatima assured him she already checked, but did not mention the Lira.

"Who are you?" he shouted at Asma.

She flinched, but didn't say anything. Fatima could smell the familiar smell of alcohol on his breathe. She had foolishly let herself hope that it would be different outside of Syria, and then her hopes only increased when he didn't drink on Moria. But the reality was this problem had followed them, and she braced herself for what else would come.

"We should have left her in Greece. She would have been better off," Fatima said under her breath. Saad glared at her and she didn't say another word.

In Belgrade, Saad began shouting at Asma once again. Fatima told him to leave her alone and that he was drunk. But he lunged toward Asma, who was standing right next to Rima. Fatima placed herself between them. With one fluid motion, Saad backhanded her and she fell. Asma and Rima both began to cry, and Fatima hushed them, singing them the same lullaby she did when they were fearful.

Thousands of refugees took shelter at the Keleti train station in Budapest. With the first clean water readily available in what seemed like weeks, Fatima stripped and bathed the girls under the spring water. Both shrieked with delight, just as other children did around them. It was then that Fatima discovered the folded picture of London Tower bridge in Asma's pocket, but she thought nothing of it and put it back.

Saad had met some other Syrian refugees and had quickly disappeared into the night. Fatima didn't mind, as the station was well lit and a sympathetic woman had offered the edge of a blanket for the girls to sleep on. It was the safest and cleanest Fatima had felt in months.

Rima had developed a croup-like cough so Fatima insisted the stop the journey for a few days. Saad relented and found a makeshift camp outside of Vienna. He once again disappeared, and to Fatima's surprise, he didn't sleep all day the following day. Instead, he took Asma to the city center where he had her beg for money while he stole wallets off the tourists.

"One day, I will teach you how to steal. I am a teacher, after all." He laughed a devious laugh. That was the first time that Asma wondered whether he really was a real teacher.

That night, he proceeded to spend all the money on alcohol, and beat Fatima for no reason whatsoever. Those in the makeshift camp had their own hardships, so no one interfered. Fatima never cried; she simply did what needed to be done to keep moving forward. In every major city they now went through, Saad took Asma to the busier areas to panhandle, and he would prey on the more distracted passersby. He even stole off their fellow refugees. Fatima saw him rob a sleeping man once and whispered, "They will kill you if you are caught." It was one thing to lift wallets off the tourists and urbanites, but to steal from your own could result in swift and severe justice; these people had nothing left to lose.

Asma still didn't say much as they moved across Europe, yet Fatima would still have entire conversations with her. She told Asma about her own childhood, her dreams for Rima and how things would be better when they reached Scotland. She would ask Asma's opinion on things and wait for a nod or grimace. One time, Asma grimaced at Saad and he raised his hand as if he was going to hit her. When she recoiled, he laughed and gave her an unwelcome hug, and said he would never hurt her.

AHMED BACK
IN LONDON

2015

Ahmed was always cold. It wasn't only the damp London weather; it was if his soul had disappeared along with his family. He became the type of doctor anyone dreaded to have: cold and sharp. His bedside manner had always been considered clinical, but now it had further deteriorated into just plain rudeness. It felt cruel to him to be saving lives, when the only lives he really cared about were gone. He was awarded the position over Dr. Stevens, but in acknowledgment, Ahmed only nodded once, shook the man's hand and left the room. He wondered if they had awarded it to him out of sheer pity, having seen him return battered and broken from Turkey.

Life went on around him, but it was if he was only

watching. He worked and slept, occasionally reminding himself to eat. Well-meaning coworkers tried to help, but were met with only coldness. There was simply no warmth left in him.

Ahmed had tried to hire a private detective but he too came up with no answers. The police officer had been correct in that a boat had sunk, but the Greek navy had estimated that they were only able to locate about half of the bodies of those who went into the sea. Those they did recover were buried in an unmarked grave. Ahmed went so far as to ask if he could have the bodies exhumed and reburied, but this request was deemed outlandish, even though he offered to cover the expense. The detective did spend months in Turkey searching, all to no avail. The man knew what Ahmed refused to accept, and after six months, he could no longer accept Ahmed's money. Ahmed sought out others, but once they heard the story their faces would drop and they would decline the offer. He called every friend and foe alike in Syria, but still he found no news.

Ahmed couldn't go back to Syria; there was nothing for him there. His exhaustive searches of Turkey proved his family was not there either. Every night, in the mere moments before sleep would take hold, he would play the "what if" game in his head. What if he had never left? What if he heard what Safia had really been saying when she told him she was scared for her and the children?

His concerned coworkers didn't limit themselves to just offering home cooked meals or invites to go out. After six months, Ahmed was approached by the hospital administration, who politely urged him to take some time off. But underneath this, he could sense what they were really saying: that in his current state, they did not feel comfortable having him operate. And like all things, Ahmed simply nodded and walked away. No emotion was left in him. He had no more tears to cry. As he stood waiting for the bus to go home, he watched the world swirl around him, unaware that his name was being called. It wasn't until Dr. Kaufman tapped him the back that he noticed the man next to him.

"My wife is cooking dinner tonight. Please come." Dr. Kaufman's voice was nearly pleading.

Ahmed was about to refuse, but Dr. Kaufman had already begun to walk away. "I will pick you up at six," he called back.

Ahmed was not in the mood for a dinner party; he could simply not answer the door that evening, but he didn't have the energy to resist. "Okay," he said quietly, but Dr. Kaufman was too far away to have heard.

***

Dr. George Kaufman and his wife, Grace, lived in a comfortable townhouse across from a park in one of London's finer neighborhoods. Ahmed couldn't get past how large it seemed. With the park across the street, it was the perfect home for a family, and he wondered if there was similar one for sale. And then it hit him again, like a wave, that he had no family. But he didn't know that for sure... This was the familiar dance in his head. Was it only realistic to let go, or was it the move of a coward to give up on his family when he didn't know for sure what had happened to them?

When George had told Grace about Ahmed, she had insisted that he bring him for dinner. George warned her that Ahmed was clinically depressed, and no matter how good Grace's cooking was, it wouldn't fix it. Her response was that home cooking and kindness did not hurt anyone, followed by a look that told him she would not take no for an answer. Grace, for all her time spent in England, was American through and through, and her stubbornness was one of the reasons George had fallen in love with her. The corn-fed midwestern brunette was unlike anyone else he had ever met, and it had been love at first sight. She had been on a study abroad program when he first met her as a medical student at Bartholomew College in London. She never returned to Iowa.

It was an enjoyable dinner, even if George and Grace did most of the talking, but there was something about Grace that was warm and kind. After dinner, she preemptively thanked George for doing the dishes. He laughed, but she reminded him that if she cooked, that meant he cleaned. He began to gather up the dishes, and Ahmed stood to help, but Grace insisted that he was a guest and she wouldn't allow it. Besides, she added, she "had to do something to keep George humble."

Grace and Ahmed made small talk, both dancing around the subject of his family. When she inquired where he was living, Ahmed explained he was renting a room to save money till his family arrived, and with that bombshell, an uncomfortable silence hung in the air.

"George told me you plan to stay in London long term," she said, trying to move the conversation on swiftly. "I know there is a nice place on the other side of the park. I saw it online and those bathrooms are the stuff of dreams." She said the last bit extra loud so George would hear over the din of him loading the dishwasher.

"Oh," Ahmed said, not entirely interested, but doing his best to be kind.

"You know, I have been dying to go see it. George hates that sort of thing and he said you had some time off," she said, deftly avoiding any mention of why he had time off.

"Maybe."

Once George returned, the conversation shifted once again to medical stuff and hospital gossip. The night came to an end, and when Ahmed went to put on his coat, Grace insisted they would drive him back. He declined her offer.

When Ahmed said goodnight one last time and closed the door, George turned to Grace. "I know what you are doing."

"What?" She grinned sheepishly.

"You cannot fix this."

"I am not trying to fix anything. But anyone would be depressed all alone in new city. Especially in a rented room that, judging by his overcoat, smells like beets."

George burst out laughing.

Four days later, Ahmed was staring at the water stain on the ceiling of his room, trying to determine if it looked more like a rabbit or elephant. The time off was meant to be a blessing, but it had only been two days and it felt like a curse. At least when he was at work, it occupied his mind. His phone rang. He looked at the screen but didn't recognize the number.

"Ahmed, hey. It's Grace."

"Hi." At first, Ahmed was simply confused why she was calling, but then he also wondered how she had his number at all.

"Are you busy today?"

"No, I was … um.." He glanced around the room to find something plausible to finish that sentence, with but he needn't bother. Grace had already continued speaking.

"Great, remember that house I was telling you about? I made an appointment to look at it this afternoon. Can you make it?"

He agreed to go for reasons he couldn't really explain.

"Great. I'll pick you up in an hour."

Grace was relentless in all the best ways possible. She brought Ahmed back to life. He no longer felt cold through and through. Not only did she help him find and furnish a home, she helped him build a community. It was Grace, who to Ahmed's surprise was a member of the Royal Astronomical Society, who re-introduced Ahmed to the subject he had loved since he was a child and how Nadir had gotten his name. She even sponsored his membership. The members-only library became a place of solitude for him, the space Ahmed would go to hide from the world.

The dull ache never left him, but a year or so after that first dinner party, it no longer pained him to laugh or live again. It was an uneasy peace, and on long nights when sleep was evasive, he would think of his beautiful family. But these thoughts were now of happy times, bittersweet to be sure, but the sting of sorrow had begun to drift away.

Grace and George had now started inviting single women to their almost-weekly dinner parties. It was the world's least subtle attempt to find someone new for him, and though he had rejoined the living, Ahmed was not sure he would ever be ready for that.

JERUSALEM

1968

C haya and Eli moved to Nachlaot, not far from Vera and Yossi. It made for a longer commute to the hospital, as the ophthalmology department didn't move to Mount Scopus but stayed in Ein Kerem, but Eli didn't mind. Louis sent a wedding present that more than covered the down payment on the two-story stone house with a lovely courtyard that Chaya immediately filled with plants. It was decidedly too large a house for only the two of them but they both hoped they would grow into it.

Eli was the happiest he could ever remember being. It was a feeling that made him nervous, as it was also the first time he had something he was scared to lose. And soon, there would be children. Hopefully, his home would be as full as Yossi's. Yossi and Vera were always insisting that, should the young couple want to give it a trial run, they were more than welcome to "borrow" their youngest daughter, a baby girl that had surprised them after they already had four children. Vera had thought she was beyond the age of having children but Noa had been a wonderful surprise. Chaya adored that baby, and Vera welcomed the help. Noa was a regular fixture in the Bronstein household.

The plan would be to try to conceive for one year, and after that, they would pursue adoption. It did not take that long: three months after their wedding, Chaya was overjoyed to find out she was expecting. Without a mother to ask all the questions, she went to Vera. She had been around children most of her life, but there were still more intimate details that she did not wish to ask publicly.

Eli felt as if he was standing on a precipice. All he could see was how quickly it could all go wrong. He began having nightmares of his time during the war, though he couldn't be certain whether the things he was dreaming of were real or a figment of his imagination. He confided in Yossi, who couldn't answer for him, but he did assure him that all new fathers had anxiety.

When the letter from France arrived, Eli knew what it was immediately. The envelope had been hastily written and was post marked from Paris. He felt as though he had been expecting this news for a while, and when he noticed that the penmanship was not that of Louis' elegant scroll of letters, it was only confirmed all the more. Louis had insisted he would never live in Paris again, so, as he stood in the entry-way, still wearing his coat and hat , he tore open the letter.

"*Dr. Bronstein, I regret to inform you of the pass-ing of Louis Dufort. As his solicitor, I request you come to Paris with regards to his estate. While there is no urgency, please know I will be leaving the city in August.*"

It was signed, but through his tears Eli could hardly make out what it said. Also included were a tele-phone number and the address in Paris. Chaya grabbed the letter but as she didn't read French, Eli had to explain to her that Louis had died. He had known the man was frail, but even in his last letter Louis had only positive things to say. First Ben and now Louis. Chaya sat next to Eli as he cried. . She cried too, but her heartbreak was for Eli.

After much back and forth, Eli headed to Paris. He did not think it was a good time to leave Chaya, but she insisted that "we will be fine," as she placed her hand on her stomach, which had only begun to show. When that did little to persuade him, Vera also assured Eli that she would keep a watchful eye. Besides, she chided, she knew better what to watch for than any man. And so, with the promise to return in three days, Eli left for Paris.

Paris seemed different than the last time. The novelty of seeing it for the first time since a child had worn off, and the sad circumstances that brought him here did little to improve his impression of it. He longed to get back to Jerusalem and Chaya as soon as possible. Perhaps Louis was right. Paris had too many ghosts.

The solicitor was an uncomfortably short man with a balding head and a curt demeanor that, Eli could only guess, was the byproduct of a defense mechanism. There was no warmth to this man and none to be found in his office. Even though Eli himself was French too, there was something about the way the Parisians viewed him and spoke to him, as if they knew he didn't belong. The solicitor used this same tone when speaking to him. Eli perched on a wooden chair that rocked ever so slightly due to one short leg. The mahogany desk and marble floor would have seemed luxurious and decadent, but the light was wrong and the room was unnaturally cold.

"I came as soon as I was able—" He began to explain but was cut off.

"Yes, yes. You're Israeli, no?" The man nodded as he looked for a folder of papers in his drawer. He had long thin fingers that reminded him of a spider. Eli knew he was being unfair, but there was something about this man that bothered him to his core.

"What of the funeral? Your letter did not say..." Eli said, trying to sound humble rather than accusatory.

"That is how Monsieur Dufort wanted it!" he snapped. "But if you must know, he is buried in the church yard in Sangette. Ahh, here is the file." He slapped the papers on his desk and began to flip through the pages.

Eli sat silently while the man looked through them.

"Monsieur Dufort," he began, once he had found what he was looking for, "as he had no other living relatives, has bequeathed to you, Dr. Elijah Bronstein, the entirety of his estate, including his home in Sangette and an account at Société Générale. I simply need your signature on these documents."

He shoved paperwork in front of Eli.

"What about the flat in Paris?" It was only after the words had left his mouth that it occurred to him that it may have come across as sounding greedy. Eli thought to apologize, but didn't.

"He sold the flat in 1963 to cover some unexpected expense. And then he also withdrew the bulk of the money a few months back. Therefore, the account balance is not substantial."

Eli knew that the "unexpected expenses" had been his tuition, and the later withdrawal had been the down payment on his and Chaya's home. He had attempted several times to pay Louis back, but the man never accepted the money.

Eli scribbled his name on the pages in front of him, and stood to leave.

"Wait, he also left this for you" In the clutches of the unpleasant man's hand, was a letter and a and small packet. Eli immediately recognized Louis' perfect penmanship.

He grabbed the letter and the packet, within which Eli could feel were keys. The man peered over his desk with a quizzical expression. Eli knew that he wanted to know why Louis would leave a seaside home and a small sum of money to, seemingly, a perfect stranger, but he made no move to open the sealed letter. It was intended to be read privately.

"Should you wish to sell the home in Sangette, please be in touch. The estate will pay for the caretaker until you decide," he said before Eli walked out.

Away from the presence of that horrid little man, Eli exhaled deeply. It was only outside that he really grasped the fact that Louis had left him everything. He had not been naive enough to think that the man would not have left him something, but he never imagined to be named his sole heir. Aside from the three months Eli has spent with him in Sangette, and one trip to Israel, Eli was a virtual stranger to him.

As he strolled through the streets of Paris and into a park, he thought for a moment. He should have brought Chaya with him. Paris, after all, is the city of love. He found a sunny spot on a bench and pulled Louis' letter from his pocket. He took a couple of deep breathes and tore it open.

"*My dearest Elijah,*
        As I write this, I know my time is near, and should

you be reading this, it will mean I have since left this earth. Perhaps where I am going I will find peace. I have left this with my lawyer as I am too much of coward to have told you the truth to your face.

Every word I told you about your mother was true. Even as an old man my heart still aches for her. I loved her with every fiber of my being, the way you love your Chaya. There is no ounce of regret in me for loving her, even if she couldn't return my feelings.

But I do face my death with many regrets, not for what I did but for what I didn't do. I believe it was your fourth birthday in 1940, a cold but sunny day that is forever etched in my soul. You father asked me for a large sum of money so that he could emigrate with you and Hannah. I laughed and assured him, with all the wisdom of man in his twenties, that France would remain untouched. He reminded me that your mother was foreign, having been born in Germany, and war was coming. I called him a fool. I was adamant that she was a naturalized citizen. He called me an ignorant playboy. He said I was prideful and I told him he was merely jealous. More words were exchanged till it came to blows. Your mother had to stop us from pummeling each other. I remember you wailing over the commotion. I left and didn't turn back.

Five months later, Germany had invaded, and in July, Vichy began stripping anyone who had become a citizen after 1927 of their naturalization, including your mother. When I heard that foreign born Jews were being sent to internment camps, I went to your father to apologize, but it was too late. Borders were closed, visas de-

nied, citizenships revoked. Vichy simply made her, and thousands of others, no longer French. I offered to be of help, but David was convinced I had personally signed her death warrant. He slammed the door in my face. Anger once again filled the spot where humility had so briefly lived.

I saw him one last time, June 14th, 1942, Bastille Day. I was shocked when he appeared. I remember it was very late and there was a curfew that he was breaking. I scolded him until I remembered everything we had always been to one another. He explained that he had sent you and Hannah south with every last franc he had and that he needed money to join you. I assured him I would do what I could, and begged him to stay. We spent the entire night laughing over memories of better times. He told me that police had come several times looking for Hannah and how scared he was for the two of you, but the plan was to meet in small town on the coast—its name is now lost to my memory. That night it was as if we were brothers again.

On the 15th, David returned home and I was to visit Société Générale to withdraw—

Eli had to stop reading. He knew that the Vet D'hiv roundup had been the morning of the 16th. Why Louis didn't get his father the money seemed immaterial at this point. What did seem odd was why this was the first time he had ever heard that his mother was not born French. There were simply too many lies. Louis was not the benevolent friend who had paid Eli's way through school. It was guilt money, blood money, that Eli had accepted. He felt sick to his stomach. He shoved the rest of the letter in his pocket and began to walk, briskly but aimlessly.

He thought he was walking without direction until he found himself in the Marais. His mind had explored all the what ifs while his feet had directed him to his family apartment. He stood there, looking at it, trying to see the past, trying to imagine Louis and his father coming to blows. Still, he could not picture it. Did his father come here and anxiously pace, waiting for the money so he could leave? He stared at his one-time home, trying to understand how this could have happened but he could not.

He must have walked dozens of kilometers, but Eli found himself eventually back at the hotel. He called Chaya. He didn't want to tell her about the slimy solicitor or that the man he had believed to be his friend had betrayed his family when they needed him the most. He only wanted to hear her voice. But Chaya could tell something was not right. Eli said he would explain all when he returned home. In part, he didn't want to upset her, but in truth, he didn't know what to make of it all. They said their goodbyes and Eli returned to the letter.

"—as much money as I could. I was determined not to make the same mistake twice, but the teller told me that I could only withdraw 3000 Francs under the law. The Franc was worth so little, I knew it would not be enough, but the largest sum of my money was in Switzerland, untouchable, even to me. I collected what items I could to sell on the black market, but when a country is starving, diamonds are not worth so much. Still, I tried. By the time I had gathered the money, it was too late.

I was convinced that, as your father was French, he would be released, so I waited and did nothing. And like the waves of the ocean that are too powerful to fight, your father was swept away beyond rescue or reach. Did he wonder why I was delayed? Did he think I had betrayed him? It gnaws at my soul to know that he never knew that I tried.

When I came to Jerusalem I had planned to tell you this, but I couldn't. I was standing in your living room, trying to muster up my nerves when I saw on your bookshelf a stuffed bunny. You may not remember this, but I gave it to you when you were born. Hannah called it Louise as a play on Louis. Seeing that bunny in your apartment took me straight back to being around your bassinet with Hannah and David, and I knew that my shame was my burden alone. Nothing good would have come of telling you.

I do not seek forgiveness for what I did not do, but know that it was not guilt that motivated me to leave my estate to you. It is only love. Love for David, Love for Hannah and Love for you.

Louis.

Eli folded the letter and placed it back in its envelope. He packed all of his clothes and neatly buried the letter at the bottom of the suitcase. At that moment, he had never wanted to leave a place more than he wanted to leave Paris.

TANZANIA/
FRANCE

1969-1998

C haya suffered a miscarriage. Scientifically, Eli knew that his being in France had nothing to do with it, but when he saw Yossi there to pick him up at the airport rather than Chaya, he hated himself for leaving her.

Eli didn't tell Chaya about Louis' letter or the contents of the estate. He had resigned himself to selling the house so he could leave the sordid past in the past. But when Chaya had her second miscarriage later that year, she fell into a deep depression. Doctors were consulted and they learnt that, while Chaya may be able to conceive again, she would never be able to carry a child to term. Eli asked her if she wanted to go to Tel Aviv to be near to the sea, but she said that Tel Aviv only reminded her of more sorrow and unhappiness, the city reminding her of Ben.

When all options available to him had run out, Eli took a leave off work for a month, left care of the Nachlaot house to Vera and took Chaya to the seaside house in Sangette. At first, it was strange, tip-toeing around what felt like someone else's home, but it soon became to feel like the honeymoon they had never had. Eli would sit on the beach and read, while Chaya fussed in the garden. They took long walk and naps. Eli eventually told her the entire story of how the home came to be theirs, explaining why it felt wrong, but Chaya didn't see it that way. She staunchly defended Louis. He had no way of knowing what hindsight had revealed, she said.

Chaya cleaned and decluttered the house. She kept having to remind herself that it belonged to them now, as she threw away old magazines and chipped coffee cups and boots that were too small for Eli but too big for her. It was in all this cleaning that she found an old easel and some canvases. When it didn't end up in the ever-growing trash heap, Eli bought Chaya oil paints from Calais. She attempted to paint the sea, but sighed every time Eli remarked that it looked good.

"Do you want to stay?" Eli asked her one morning as they sipped their steaming hot tea over the plank-wood kitchen table.

"You mean in France?"

"You seem really happy here. I am sure I could find a job somewhere nearby. Or at least I could try."

"I hope we will come back many times, but I miss our home, and our friends. What's more, and don't argue with me, I know you love your job. Let's go home."

In Jerusalem, life resumed its normal rhythm. In Sangette, the couple decided that they would pursue adoption. The excitement of becoming a family was palpable. They filled out dozens of documents. Neither Eli or Chaya had their own birth certificates so, instead, they both used their British-signed visas from Cyprus. Eli had to procure his military record, tax forms and all his banking information. Both had to give permission for their medical records to be reviewed and to be interviewed in their home.

Before the home interview, Chaya and Vera scrubbed the house from top to bottom. Chaya had bought a new dress, but decided at the last minute that she didn't want to look like she was trying too hard so wore an old one instead. Eli laughed at this. He knew she was nervous, but there was no reason to be. She was great with children, they had a lovely home and he was more than able to provide for a child. The social worker had assured them everything looked to be in order.

Chaya watched the phone, waiting for it to ring. It did not.

When it finally did, Chaya was at Vera's, helping to

sew Purim costumes.

"Dr. Bronstein?"

"Speaking"

"This is Samuel Gilat. I work with the district court in regards to the Adoption of Children Law. Would it be possible for you to come speak with me tomorrow? Say around two?"

"Me and my wife?"

"No, only you."

Eli tried to not let his confusion show in his voice. "Of course, thank you."

This was not the happy phone call that they had been expecting. Eli wondered if he had done something wrong. Had he failed to disclose something, or forgotten a document? Why would they want to see only him? He decided not to tell Chaya of the call or of the meeting until he knew more. After the revelation that his mother was German, Eli had to wonder if there was still more to the story, something he didn't know. Sleep was impossible that night.

At the district court the following afternoon, Eli paced until Mr. Gilat invited him in. The office was teeming with paperwork, but Mr. Gilat seemed well aware of where everything was. He invited Eli to sit.

"Dr. Bronstein, I invited you here today due to the sensitive nature of what was discovered in reviewing your application for adoption."

"Mr. Gilat, I am sorry I do not understand. My wife and I provided everything you asked for."

Mr. Gilat cleared his throat. "It's in regards to your wife."

"My wife?"

"Well, you see." Mr. Gilat paused. "When we asked for medical records, we were only able to locate the ones for a Mrs. Chaya Bronstein."

Eli sat silently, still not understanding. "Yes, that is my wife."

"As I am sure you are aware, she was married previously."

"Yes, to Benjamin Rafaeli."

"Precisely."

Eli could feel his patience waning and his face beginning to flush.

"The medical records for a Mrs. Chaya Rafaeli show that she was hospitalized twice with severe mental distress. One of those times was against her will by her then husband. The hospital notes from Tel Aviv stated that she was believed to be a danger to herself or others."

"May I see them?"

Mr. Gilat handed Eli the papers. They were as he said, and at the bottom of one, was Ben's signature. Eli was surprised by the hospitalizations and the treatments, but he had seen this "mental distress," himself after her miscarriages.

"Also, the absence of her military record was noted. There is paperwork to suggest that she had a medical exemption. I imagine if we were to look under her maiden name, we might find more of the same."

Eli sadly shook his head in disbelief and as he read through the documents, he covered his lips with his fingers instinctively . He stopped reading when he saw that, amongst her treatments, were several rounds of ECT.

"As a doctor, you must know we cannot place a child in a home with this type of history. The social worker had the loveliest things to say about you and your wife. I see all the paperwork is in order, so it occurred to me that you may have been unaware of this history."

"Yes, I was unaware." Eli finally understood why Chaya hadn't been happy in Tel Aviv. Still, she should have told him, or Ben should have.

Mr. Gilat looked at Eli sympathetically, but again reiterated that they would not place a child with them. Eli thanked him for his time, grabbed his hat and left. For the rest of the afternoon, he meandered through the city. He wasn't angry with Chaya, but he wasn't certain how he would break this news to her.

Days passed without Eli saying a word. Finally, when he could not take it anymore, he sought the guidance of Vera and Yossi. He told them the entire story as they sat in Vera's kitchen late one night.

"Just tell her the truth," Yossi said, breaking the silence that had hung in the air.

"Are you out of your mind?" Vera shot back.

"Well, he has to tell her something."

"Of course he does, but not the truth."

"Are you suggesting the man lie to his wife?" Yossi asked coldly.

"Chaya has always been sensitive soul. She already blames herself for not being able to have children. What do you think it would do to her if he then tells her she is the reason they cannot adopt? Should he tell her the court thinks she'd be an unfit mother?"

"Oh no, that would be bad," Yossi said as the realization hit him.

"So, tell Chaya you are the reason they won't let you adopt," she said, staring at Eli.

Yossi let out a laugh. "I am not for lying, but if you are going to, it has to be convincing. Clean cut Dr. Eli here has no skeletons, no defects, plus they grew up together. There isn't much she wouldn't know."

"Well, we have to find something wrong with him."

"Any gambling debts?" Yossi asked.

"No."

"Ever been arrested?" Vera asked, unconvinced.

"No, I have never been arrested, and I think Chaya would have known about it."

"Or would she?" Yossi rose from the table and was clearly replaying a conversation in his mind, but it wasn't coming through his lips.

"Care to share?"

"It's a bit insane but it might work." Yossi sat back down. "So, I knew this guy—nice guy; we had some mutual friends. One day he asked me if Egged was hiring. I said I didn't know but would ask around. They were looking for something in the office and he applied for it, but he was never hired. I saw him a year or two later. He was still out of work. I asked him what happened. He told me that, when he enlisted at eighteen, he and two of his friends had been miserable so they deserted and hitchhiked to Eliat. The two friends returned a few days later to the base, but Amos didn't. He was gone thirty-five days or so before he was arrested."

Eli and Vera eyed Yossi suspiciously.

"His commander had him jailed for thirty-five days

and then he had to finish out his service. He told me it was in his military record, and that's why he wasn't hired. But his family didn't know, probably still doesn't."

"An employer is not supposed to ask for military records," Eli objected.

Yossi thought for a moment. "That's what he told me. But the adoption agency did ask for military records, so tell Chaya there was something in those. Tell her you were sent to a military prison for fist fighting or court martialed for losing your weapon—that also happened to a guy I know."

"I am not telling my wife I was a deserter."

"Of course not, but Yossi is on to something," Vera said. "Otherwise, you have to tell her the truth."

***

A few weeks later, one day when Chaya returned home from shopping, she heard Eli calling for her to come upstairs. He was in the room that was to be the nursery, but when she bounded round the corner, she saw not a bassinet but a large easel, with canvases stacked along the wall, and a chest of drawers that had jars filled with brushes and paints stacked neatly.

"Surprise!" Eli tried to sound as joyous as he could.

"But Eli—"

"Wait, there is more!" Eli handed her an envelope.

She tore it open, and read the paper inside. She smiled. "You registered me for classes at the Bezalel School of Arts?"

"You have painted every day since we were in Sangette, and I thought you would like to take a class or two for fun. If you hate it, you can quit. Here, come try out your new painting spot." He gestured to the stool in front of the easel.

She sat down and nodded; it was a nice spot. "Eli, this is so lovely, but this is meant to be the baby's room."

He knelt in front of her. Even before he spoke, the tears had welled in her eyes.

"Eli?" she asked, pleading.

Eli was now crying. "Chaya, I never told you or anyone that when I was first enlisted I got into some trouble. I was young and stupid, and I was court marshaled."

"Don't worry, I am sure no one will hold the actions of an eighteen-year-old against you now," she said reassuringly.

Eli had hoped that that was as far as the lie would have to go, but he had to double down. "I had to serve three months in a military prison."

"Oh my god, what did you do?"

"Please don't make me say. I am too ashamed." Eli buried his face in his hands, not for dramatic effect, but because he couldn't look at her when he told her the next part. "The courts found out everything, and I am so sorry, but they think I am unfit to be father."

Chaya knelt next to Eli and wept. When the tears had slowed, she rose to her feet looked at him, holding her hand out to help him up.

"So, I cannot have children, and you cannot adopt. What a pair we make!"

"I am so sorry," Eli whispered.

"There will be no more apologies from either of us for things we cannot change."

Eli waited, watching for any signs of the darkness that had enveloped her before, but there was none. Over the coming weeks, she plunged herself into her art classes. And while there was shock and sadness, all things considered, she seemed to be doing alright. There were still times when her mood would shift, but this was usually resolved by a trip to the cottage. Over the years, they'd spend a week here or there, long weekends, even a month in summer in the house by the sea. Eli never told her the truth about the adoption, and she never told him about the hospitalizations. It was the only lie he had ever told her, and perhaps the first time he understood why Louis had lied to him. Only once more did she ever ask what he did to get court marshaled, but again he said it was too shameful.

In 1971, Chaya was renting a co-op artist space in the

Old City. She had become an accomplished painter and had even sold some pieces to a gallery in New York. She had become most famous for her skylines of Jerusalem. Her career was beginning to take off, when Eli approached her with a radical idea. He was so excited, but was not sure how she we would react. Even through her success, he could see she was becoming restless.

"You know that the hospital has ophthalmology programs all over Africa? Well, they need someone to head up the program in Tanzania. Dr. Shinar has been there two years and, well, he wants to return home. They asked me if I would be interested."

"Interested in moving to Tanzania?"

Eli rocked on his heels and kept his hands in his pockets, staring at the floor like a child. "It's a two-year commitment."

"Will there be elephants?" Chaya grinned.

***

After the initial culture shock, Chaya and Eli came to love Tanzania. There were two branches of the hospital's program: training for young doctors in the capital in Dar es Salaam and a more rural hospital in a town called Moshi. As Eli was the more tenured of the two doctors and as the position in Moshi was the one being vacated, that was where they moved. The house being vacated by Dr. Shinar was large and had a huge wall around it, which made Chaya nervous, but all the houses were like this, more like compounds. The house also came with a dedicated staff: a maid, a cook and groundskeeper. Chaya said she didn't need staff, but Dr. Shinar explained that it was simply how it was done out here, and pointed out all the things that even after two years he still didn't know how to do. Chaya quickly came to see how right he had been. For example, the first time she say Laya quickly hack apart a jackfruit.

Moshi was lush and green, and the vibrant colors were the stuff of a painter's dreams. In the distance, sat Mt. Kilimanjaro. On a clear morning, Chaya could see the mountain from her porch, and she took to calling it "her mountain." The house was down a long red dirt drive that was canopied by vibrant purple Jacaranda trees, the wind making its leaves flutter around painting the road like a lilac carpet. In the winter, there were vibrant red trees that did the same. They bloomed in December and were referred to as "Christmas trees."

The summers were nearly unbearable and the winter brought the rains, but Chaya and Eli were happy. Weeks were long and stressful at the hospital. Eli saw eye diseases that had been eradicated in most parts of the world, and particularly distressing were the children who would soon become blind because of things that had not been treated. Too often, the damage had been done, and Eli could do nothing but confirm that the patient would lose their sight. Or if surgery could remedy it, most often patients couldn't afford the trip to the capital. Despite it being not allowed, Eli had paid the cost of the journey to Dar es Salaam more than once, for several children needing cataract or muscle surgery.

Eli and his assistants were the only eye doctors for hundreds of kilometers. But no matter what he had seen, he always tried to leave his stress at work, and their weekends were filled with fun. Moshi had a large expat community that embraced the newcomers, so there were always dinner parties to attend or day trips organized to coffee plantations. They spent one long weekend on the crystal beaches of Zanzibar. Neither had ever seen water like it before, and the sand felt so soft underfoot. Once back in their hotel, they fell asleep to the sound of the waves curling into one another under the mosquito netting.

True to his promise, Eli took Chaya on safari so she could see the elephants, and along with a British expat named Simon, he climbed Kilimanjaro. Eli had never felt more alive. He knew he was doing good work, and being in Africa, it felt just like the adventures his mother had told him of as a child.

Both would have considered staying, but like so many other instances in their life, politics and war got in the way. When war broke out once again in 1973, Eli was too far away to serve, but as a result of the Yom Kippur war, many African nations "uninvited" the doctors from Hadassah. Tanzania severed all ties with Israel, and Chaya and Eli had to leave. They gave tearful hugs to their new friends, overpaid the last of the staff that worked in their home and returned to Jerusalem. It would be unpatriotic to say it, but Chaya was forever grateful they had been abroad when the war started.

They lived happily in the house in Nachlaot for the next twenty-five years, but always returned to the home by the sea for respite.

SANGETTE

1998-2010

C haya was always tired. She didn't want to paint or to travel. She had no appetite. Eli was worried, but she laughed off his concerns, reminding him that they were both now old. He was sixty-two and she was sixty-one, but still Eli fussed. Unlike his wife, he still felt spritely, and could run circles around the young doctors. He was now the head of the ophthalmology department, and insisted to anyone who questioned him that he was not ready to retire yet. He walked several kilometers each day and carried himself with the demeanor of a much younger man.

Chaya, who had a fear of doctors and hospitals, had put off going for an appointment for as long as Eli would allow. But he had persuaded her to come, and now he held her hand while the doctor explained that she had breast cancer. With some aggressive treatment, the doctors believed they could beat it.

For a few years, the battle was in their favor. Chaya returned to her normal self: energetic happy, and nearly always covered in paint. As a celebrated artist, she now gave guest lectures at Jerusalem University. Her short greying hair and unique sense of style made her seem a bit of an eccentric, which only added to her popularity, both in Israel and abroad. Eli, who himself was at the top of his field, often jokingly introduced himself as Chaya Bronstein's husband.

The cancer returned, and again they fought it back. Chaya quipped that they both now practically lived at the hospital. But at the end of September 2006, the doctor told Chaya and Eli that it had spread to her bones. Eli jumped into doctor mode, asking about the options. He had an awareness of the different trials being done both at home and internationally. Chaya only squeezed his hand, and Eli knew what she was trying to tell him. The doctor excused himself from the room to let them speak privately.

"Eli, it's been eight years. I am tired."

"You cannot give up. We can beat this!" he insisted.

Chaya only shook her head. "Not this time, dear."

When the doctor returned, Chaya asked the only question she wanted an answer to. The doctor said, at best, maybe a year. The doctor explained that they could make sure she was comfortable, but beyond that, there was little that could be done medically.

Chaya thanked him, shook his hand and set about doing what needed to be done.

Eli couldn't bear the thought of being without Chaya, He put in his notice of retirement that afternoon. For every moment she had left, he wanted to be with her. Eli was now seventy, and Chaya teased that if refusing treatment was all it took for him to retire she would have done it years ago. In addition to her sense of humor, Chaya was very matter-of-fact about the entire thing. She quickly put her affairs in order: arranging the details of her studio, charging Noa with looking after the house and finally, packing for what she knew would be her final trip. She wanted to spend her last days by the sea, a fact that surprised no one.

Eli moved as if in a fog. In his seventy years, he had seen many things, but he couldn't wrap his mind around that fact that everything being done was in preparation for Chaya's death. It had never occurred to him that she would go first. He was older, though not by much. Wasn't it supposed to be the husband? He wished that it had been summer, so Chaya could have sat by the sea and painted, but it was November. Chaya cleaned out her closet, so when Eli returned he wouldn't have to go through her things. She said goodbye to their friends and their home.

Sangette was cold, and the wind off the sea harsh. Still, Chaya would take her morning coffee outside every day, letting the wind sting her face. At first, Eli set about making sure that they had enough firewood, that the car had petrol, that the sink stopped leaking, but eventually he ran out of tasks. With nothing else to do, he hovered around her, wanting to make sure she was okay, until one day, Chaya could not take it anymore, and she locked Eli out of the house. She told him to go into the village and find something to amuse himself. It was that day he met James, a local who was playing both sides of a chess game. Eli introduced himself and James properly slaughtered him in the next three games. It became a standing game every morning. Should Eli not show, James didn't take it personally, but sipped his espresso and played both sides.

Spring came, and on the days she was feeling up to it, Eli brought Chaya out to sit in the sun and she would lovingly directed him in the garden on what to pull and where to plant. It was a rare day that Chaya wanted to paint; her pain was nearly constant by this point. The doctor in Israel had made arrangements for pain medicine to be acquired through a hospital in Calais—Eli was more than capable of administering it as he was a surgeon—but Chaya refused had until the pain became unbearable.

One morning, Eli woke, startled to find that Chaya was not next to him. He sprung to his feet, but breathed out a sigh of relief when he saw her on the patio in the summer sun, painting.

"Good morning."

"Good morning." Chaya smiled. "You were sleeping so

soundly, I didn't want to wake you."

"That is beautiful," Eli said, looking at the sea scape on her canvas.

"I still cannot get the waves correct." She sighed and laid down her brush. "Are you going to meet James for chess this morning?"

"I think I will stick close to the house," he said, attempting to sound nonchalant about the whole thing.

"Really, I will be fine for a few hours. Go on."

Eli plucked a rose from the garden and presented it to her before leaving. He took a shower, shaved and then walked into the village. They had bought a second-hand car to use, but Eli preferred walking. In Israel, they had never owned a car, and besides, the sea air was warm and salty. He sat at the cafe and took out James in two out of three of their matches. James knew Chaya was nearing the end, but it had become an unspoken understanding that Eli did not want to talk about it. He came to the cafe to play chess so as not to face the inevitable for a few hours each day. But Eli could tell James felt bad, as over the last two weeks, he had insisted on buying Eli's coffee.

When he returned home, Chaya was in bed sleeping. Eli sat next to her and watched her as she dozed. Her eyes fluttered and she struggled to wake herself. She reached out for Eli. He grabbed her hand in both of his. Chaya smiled.

"Even as children, you always reached out for me when you knew I was frightened. You've been holding my hand since the day we met."

"I may have wanted to, but I did not hold your hand the day we met."

Chaya let out a soft laugh. "You don't remember? Sam and Talia had met us at the port, they put us in car and you were next to me. I couldn't understand what was being said. It was dark, and I was so scared that I was shaking. And then you reached out in the dark and you held my hand."

Eli tried to see it in his mind, but he couldn't. But he did suppose that it had always been his instinct to protect her.

"During the war, you held my hand. It was you holding my hand the day Ben died, the day we were married, the days we lost our babies." Tears were rolling down her face.

Eli kissed her forehead, fighting back his own tears.

"Please don't let go now," she whispered.

"I won't let go." He squeezed her hand.

Eli sat next to her for hours. The sun had gone down and yet he didn't move. He stayed until her breathing stopped, and even then he sat next to her for a long time still, holding her hand. He wasn't ready to say goodbye, but eventually it came time to move. A single phone call put things into motion. Chaya had already made all the arrangements; everything had been decided.

She had apologized profusely because, though she had wanted to spend her last days by the sea, she wanted to be buried in Jerusalem. But she had arranged everything so precisely, all Eli had to do was take her home one last time. As she was loaded onto the plane, he watched on through the airport windows. If it had been allowed, he would have flown sitting next to her casket.

He said his last goodbye on a day that Chaya would have loved: it was sunny and warm, the white stones of the cemetery nearly blinding. It seemed fitting that her grave was on a hill with an amazing view of the city, as she was an artist known for her skylines of Jerusalem. Vera and Yossi, both now in their eighties, as well as their children and grandchildren, stood in the blistering heat next to Eli to say goodbye. Students Chaya had taught, and doctors Eli had worked with from the hospital all attended, but Eli felt truly alone in a way he never had before.

The city was not the same without her. Nothing was the same without her. The house that was always too big for the two of them now felt cavernous. There were half-finished canvases that he didn't know what to do with, yet he couldn't bring himself to throw them away. A friend suggested that he sell the house and move into an apartment, and went to see one of the new buildings, but it felt cold, soulless even, and there were no memories there.

Yossi died the following year, and their oldest son and his family moved in to their home to help care for Vera. Vera's health was declining rapidly, and when Yossi passed, Eli was convinced that Vera would soon follow. In 2010, Vera passed away. From that point, Eli saw nothing left for him in Jerusalem.

He left the house to Noa, who, in so many ways, had been the daughter Chaya never had. She insisted that she couldn't accept it, but Eli explained that it would have been what Chaya wanted. The only thing he asked of her in return was that, when his time came, to please see that he was laid to rest next to Chaya. He would spend whatever time he had left by the sea. Some of his best memories of Chaya were in that cottage. And should he ever miss Jerusalem, he took three of her paintings with him—his favorite, a painting of a stone alleyway in the Old City, as that is how he would always remember his home.

FATIMA FLEES

2015

Saad promised that once they reached Scotland, everything would be better, but as they continued along the road, it felt as though it was becoming longer, and things were becoming worse. The weather was turning and none of them had the proper attire for the early fall nights. Any money that Saad stole went to alcohol, and when he caught Fatima attempting to take some in order to buy food, he beat her severely.

Rima's cough had grown worse, but Saad seemed unbothered by it. By September, the family had made it as far as Paris. Fatima wished to stay, but Saad made it clear that his cousin was waiting. He assured Fatima that soon they would reach a lovely home, with his cousins and it would finally be a place of safety. Fatima clung to this dream for as long as she could, but as time passed, it felt more and more like a mirage.

"Besides, we have to return this princess to her father." Saad chuckled, nodding toward Asma.

"We don't know how to find him, and that's even if he is still in London. We cannot be sure he is even alive."

"Don't be a fool!" Saad hissed. "It took us every cent we had and I still had to steal in order to cross. How does a single mother of two afford passage *and* life jackets? If we find her father, she is our golden ticket. If not, I am sure there are other ways we can benefit."

Fatima didn't ask what he meant by "other ways," but she could feel her skin crawl at the thought of it. There were simply no good ways to make money off an orphaned child. Fatima had tried several times along the journey to leave Asma—it was the only thing she could do—but every time Saad found out, he went back and retrieved her. And yet, when Fatima thought things couldn't get any worse, they did.

It was on the final night in Paris. Rima coughed throughout the night, and Saad was attempting to sleep off his drunken stupor in the makeshift shelter that Fatima had erected with a tarp. Annoyed at the incessant coughing, he screamed at Fatima to make Rima stop so he could sleep. She rocked her and paced with her in her arms, but it did little to soothe Rima, who, if Fatima had to guess, had pneumonia. Saad rose and screamed in Fatima's face.

She apologized and said she was doing all she could, but the baby needed a doctor.

"We don't have money for a doctor!" he screamed, even though he was standing only inches from her face.

"We would if you didn't drink it all away," she shot back before she thought it through.

Saad began to hit her, and in turn, Rima, who was still her arms. Fatima curled herself around the baby to protect her, but both had already sustained blows. When Saad had exhausted himself, he stepped away and went back to sleep. The next morning, before leaving for the crossing to England, Saad brought the family into a pharmacy and purchased medicine. Beyond that, Saad acted as if nothing had happened, and Fatima said not one word of it.

The plan was to take either the train or the ferry into the UK, and once in London, Saad's cousin would meet them and take them onwards to Edinburgh. But, like the thousands of others who had made it as far as Calais, they found the border closed. It was all due to something called The Schengen Agreement, which the UK had opted out of, resulting in the bottleneck of refugees at the port. Saad assured Fatima that there must be a way to cross, that they would only be in Calais for a few days.

When fall came, the family was still in the camp known as "the jungle." Fatima soon understood how it came to have such a moniker. The camp was in a disused landfill. It was cold and dirty, lacking even the most basic of sanitation, but unlike most of the other camps they had been in, this one was not made up mostly of other Syrians, but of Afghans and Sudanese. It was also filled primarily with young men, who often, out of sheer frustration or boredom, would get into massive fights, each group siding with their own and joining in the fray. The local papers would call it gang violence, but the only loyalty was by nationality. And similar to most gangs, the camp was well stocked with vices: gambling, alcohol and prostitutes.

Illegal passage into the UK could be bought for an incredible sum. Saad's cousin sent money that was meant to be saved toward this, but it never lasted more than a day or so. Saad refused to apply for asylum in France as he insisted that they would make it to the UK. As time dragged on, the idea of a lovely home in Scotland drifted further from Fatima's mind. All she could see was the dirt and the cold, the bruises that had become her daily torment. When whispers came about the camp being cleared, she once again urged Saad to return to Paris and apply for asylum, but he would not hear of it. He said the rumor was only that: a rumor.

Fatima did what she could to sustain the family, but she knew that winter would be coming. The winds of the north sea routinely destroyed their hastily constructed shelters . Fatima fought bitterly when Saad received the largest sum of money yet from his cousin. She insisted that Rima and Asma needed warmer clothes and food, But Saad dismissed her concerns, saying that he was saving it for their crossing to the UK.

The fight escalated, and for once, Fatima did not relent. And when Saad slapped her, she did not cry out, but simply stood there, stone-faced, defiant, still making her demands. Saad slapped her again and still she did not let a single tear fall. When that failed, Saad backhanded Rima, who then wailed. Fatima scooped her up and Saad grinned. She had never seen him hit Rima before, not intentionally at least.

That night, when Saad returned and passed out, Fatima slipped the last of the money from his pocket. She grabbed a sleeping Rima, shushing her in her arms, and before she snuck from the tent, she went over to a sleeping Asma.

She kissed her on her head and whispered, "I pray you can forgive me one day. May Allah bless you."

Asma's eyes fluttered open, but on seeing Fatima's face, she drifted back to sleep. Fatima didn't look back as she slipped into the night. She gave the man all the money she had stolen, and some more she had been able to siphon from Saad before then. She got in the truck with Rima, and watched the darkness pass by as they disappeared into the night.

Had Fatima been able to afford it, she would have taken Asma too, but she only had enough for her and Rima. She was glad that she had taken the time to tell the child what she must do: that when the camp was emptied, she would need to be very brave and tell them that Saad was not her father. The girl had nodded, and Fatima prayed that when that day came, she would find her voice. In the back of the truck, Fatima cried, but deep down she knew she could not save them all.

When Saad woke to find her gone, he screamed at Asma who said nothing. Exasperated, he left under the guise of looking for them, and when he didn't return that night, Asma had to go out herself to look for food. She had been told not to leave the tent alone, but she remembered begging in the city centers, and thought she knew what she must do. In desperation, she began pillaging gardens, but found that most things had already been harvested. Each night, she would venture further and further out until she came across a lovely house with a garden that still had carrots and other vegetables.

Each day, she would return to the camp to sleep. Sometimes Saad would be there, sometimes he wouldn't, but for the most part, their paths rarely crossed. When he did return, it was often late at night while she was out, on her way to find food. This suited Asma fine, as with Fatima and Rima gone, she didn't want to become the object of his rage.

Asma had been returning to the same garden almost every night, and each time there would be a small basket filled with fruits and vegetables. Then, bottles of water began to appear.

Tensions were running high in the camp, with rumors of its closure becoming more and more rampant. People who were desperate to cross to the UK were beginning to take unprecedented risks, drowning while attempting to stow away on the ferry, or getting hit by trains or trucks using the channel tunnel. This desperation boiled over into more fights, and it was the first time Asma had seen Saad bloodied and bruised. Though, despite what appeared to be very nasty injuries, she felt no sympathy for him.

What Fatima hadn't known was that it was not only her own fate she would change by stealing the money. Saad had been drawn into gambling with an Afghani, to whom he owed everything Fatima had stolen and then some. The beating had been a warning, but with no more money and a nasty temper, Saad found himself facing death or having to leave the jungle. He attempted to flee one night, but was stopped. Then he disappeared once and for all. When his body washed ashore, he was classified as yet another desperate refugee who had tried to cross the channel and drowned.

EMPTYING THE CAMP

2015

"They are emptying the camp," James said nonchalantly, as he took one of Eli's pawns.

"Emptying?"

"Yeah, that's what I heard."

"Emptying? But to where?"

"I don't know, but it is your move."

Eli was too distracted to play anymore. He made a horrible move, knowing it would leave the queen vulnerable.

"Check mate," James said, not noticing that Eli's mind was somewhere else.

It had been a month since the incident with the "rabbit." Eli had watched patiently each night, as like
clockwork, the girl appeared. Eli would whisper to
himself as he sat in the dark, "No, don't take the carrots. They aren't grown yet," or "Take the kale. It's
perfectly ripe."

The child had no knowledge of this, though, and continued to forage through his garden without mercy,
digging up entire plants that weren't ready. Had
Chaya been alive, she would have gone out to the
child, offering her a meal or whatever else she may
need. But Chaya was not alive, and Eli considered his
produce as enough. At least, that is what he told himself, but the truth was, he was afraid that if he spoke
to her, he would scare the child away.

After many nights, protesting internally without
making a noise, Eli began to pick the ripe fruit and
vegetables, and leave them in a small wicker basket. The plan worked, and the girl stopped pillaging
through his neatly planted rows, and began to take
what was inside the basket. And Eli had been content
with this relationship, up until just a moment ago,
when James told him that the camp was to be emptied. Perhaps it was nothing more than his own curiosity, but Eli wanted to see who had sent the little
girl to steal, though it was the very reason the other
townsfolk like James were eager to see the camp demolished.

Knowing his old legs would not keep up with that of

a child's, he started in the middle of the route he assumed she would take, and he was right. One moonless night, he waited in his car, and he watched as the child passed him, oddly enough, on the way to his house. Then he watched as she returned the way she came, her tattered shopping bag filled with the goods from the basket. He slipped out of his car and silently closed the door, then, staying as far back as he could while still being able to see her Eli followed. It had struck him as odd that she was indeed alone. He'd presumed that someone must have accompanied her part of the way. Coming upon the camp—though "camp" was a loose term; it was more of a shanty town, with houses constructed out of anything that would stand—he tightened the gap between them.

Following perhaps a bit too closely, he watched her tuck herself into what couldn't even be referred to as a tent, rather a tarp held up by four tilted posts. There were no doors or any protection from the elements. A mild gust of wind would easily rip the makeshift awning from the sticks that were planted in the mud. It was only because of the dark that Eli couldn't see in, to see whom the child had come back to.

Eli had heard rumors of violence in the camp, but he didn't believe most of it. However, he still deemed it better to come back in the daylight to see for himself. He wanted to know who would send a child so far in the dead of night. As he turned to go, his mind no longer occupied by the pursuit of the child, the stench hit him. It was like a wave crashing onto rocks. Eli gagged, remembering that smell from his own childhood. Walking quickly to exit the camp, he realized his shoes were covered in not only mud, but human excrement. The camp was darker than he had imagined, and even as decently built, albeit old, man, Eli didn't feel safe. He wondered how the child did it—or maybe that was why she came in the dead of night.

Eli took off his shoes, leaving them by the side of the road before getting into his car. It was only in hindsight that he realized he should have kept them for the following day. He told himself that he was crazy, that he didn't need to go back, that he didn't need to know who was stealing. It didn't matter. But as if drawn by a gravitational pull, the next day he found himself walking to the camp. The sunlight had only increased the rancid smell, and this time it wasn't quiet; humanity was everywhere he looked: men stood trying to sell Eli what might have been stolen goods, women were about cooking and washing clothes in already dirty water, and kids were running around after a deflated soccer ball.

As much as the scene before him assaulted his senses, Eli was also a curiosity in the camp. They all knew that this well-dressed Frenchman had no business being there. He followed the same way he had gone the night before, and soon found the small child under the tarp structure. She was even smaller in the daylight. Her long black hair was matted and her hands black from the dirt. But she was alone.

Truly alone. Unlike the other makeshift structures he passed, there was no woman bustling about, no man lounging inside, no other children around her. Eli stood watching her sleep far longer than he probably should have, his eyes landing on the empty shopping bag next to her that had been filled the night before.

Eli had always known there were children alone in the camp, but he had assumed that they were older —children, yes, but more like teenagers. Could it be possible that this child was all alone? She was far too young. From her size, Eli guessed that she couldn't have been more than six or seven.

Weaving his way through the camp, he made his way into a tent that had been set up by one of the various charities that provided aid. Grabbing the attention of young blonde women, he began to ask a question, but it came out more like a confused statement.

"There is a little girl alone."

The woman stared at him for a moment, waiting for him to explain more. When he didn't, she gave him a pitying look.

"There are a lot of children alone here."

"Well, she is very young."

"And?" the woman said, raising an eyebrow.

"Well, do something. Isn't that why you do-gooders are here?"

"Look around." The woman's tone was more biting than she intended. "There are ten thousand people here. Over one thousand are unaccompanied children. This is the largest refugees crisis since World War Two. And see that woman over there?" she said, pointing to a slightly overweight but kindly-looking brunette. "It is only me, her and one other. We simply don't have the means to help them all. In fact, there is very little we can do at this point. There is no police presence in camp, so the children are especially vulnerable to crime and human trafficking." She said all this while cutting open palates of bottled water. Eli counted that there were ten palates. Even if each held a hundred bottles of water, he reasoned that the woman was right; the sheer volume the camp had grown to made it impossible to offer any effective aid.

He had been standing in silence, but he finally interjected. "But what will happen to them when the camp is emptied?"

The woman pushed away a piece of hair that had come loose from her ponytail, and looked up from the palates.

"I don't know."

Eli thanked her, and before she looked up, he was gone.

That night, he sat silently in the garden. He didn't want to scare the child, but perhaps he could get her to an orphanage. Had Chaya been alive, he could easily play out the argument that would have ensued: Eli insisting that she couldn't just keep a stray child, and Chaya responding with an assertive, "watch me." But Eli was still right; he couldn't keep this child.

That night, the girl appeared again, as expected, though it was later than usual. Eli almost feared she wouldn't have come. What if something happened to her? He shouldn't have become this invested, he thought, as he berated himself. He kept telling himself that she was being sent to steal by those too lazy or cowardly to do it themselves. But deep down, he knew this couldn't be true. And still, he waited.

The child froze when she saw Eli. He smiled in attempt to reassure her that he presented no danger, but she didn't move. He bent down to wicker basket and grabbed an apple. Truth be told, his garden didn't produce as much as the child had needed, so he had started to supplement the basket with some produce from the market. He didn't even have apple trees, though he assumed correctly that the child wouldn't have noticed this. He held out the apple to the child.

Asma considered him carefully. He didn't seem angry that she had been stealing, and in fact, it looked like he was offering her more. She had become a very good —and more importantly a fast—judge of character.

"Eli." he said, patting himself

"Asma," she said, grinning.

"Well, it's nice to meet you, Asma."

THE MEETING

2015

Eli and Asma stood, staring at one another, neither sure what to do next. Eli indicated for her to follow him and she did, albeit warily. He turned on all the lights on the patio and gestured for her to sit.

Asma was unsure, but the man seemed kind and he *had* been leaving her food, so she sat down. He lifted his hand to his mouth—the international sign of asking whether she wanted to eat. Eli had to hide his disgust at how dirty and skinny she was.

Eli disappeared into the kitchen, but left the back door open as he rummaged through his cabinets, trying to find something to make for her to eat. Having been a bachelor for so long, his culinary skills were lacking, but he began to make scrambled eggs, and toast, with Nutella.

Asma hovered by the back door, watching him cook. Her mouth salivating as the smell of the eggs wafted through the air. When he was ready to bring the plate back to her on the patio, he turned around to see her already sitting at the kitchen table. Eli smiled as he laid it in front of her and she attacked the meal with such fury, he was afraid it would all reemerge. He kept saying, "slowly, slowly." But Asma devoured it in seconds.

When she was done, they sat there in silence. Asma stood up and began to walk through the house, running her small but dirty fingers over books and trinkets. She stopped when she came across the stuffed bunny and stared at it for a long time.

Eli noticed. "Oh, that's Louise. She is an old friend," he said as he handed it to her, who then hugged it fiercely. Eli had to stop a tear from falling. She continued wandering about the house, carrying Louise as she went, and stopped in front of one of Chaya's paintings. It was the one of the stone alleyway in the Old City.

"Syria," Asma exclaimed, though the way she said it, it sounded more like *su-ria*.

Since Ben's death, Eli had harbored an ill will to all thing Syrian, but at this moment, that was the furthest thing from his mind.

"Jerusalem," Eli said. Asma didn't respond to this but, she continued to stare at it. Eli could imagine that there was probably somewhere in Syria that looked similar. He tried to speak to her in French, but Asma didn't respond. Nor did English provoke any kind of response.

Eli tried to remember what Arabic he could. It was rusty at best, but he was able to ask Asma about her mother and father. The words very similar to those in Hebrew.

"Oum?"

Asma sadly shook her head.

"Baba?"

Asma took the well-worn postcard and handed it to Eli. He looked it over, but didn't understand. How could her father be in London and she be alone? What kind of man would leave his child alone in the camps? The townspeople had been complaining about them for ages, each one of them had apparently had something "stolen," and they said crime would continue to rise as long as the camp was still here. Eli had tried to stay out of it, but the reputation was appalling. He cursed the Syrians under his breath once more, but then he thought of his own past, his own experience with camps. Had the family been separated? Had they planned to meet in London? He couldn't be sure.

While he was rolling the possibilities through his mind, and then telling himself why that was improbable, Asma somehow disappeared. He scanned the room but didn't see her. He had assumed she had left, but when he turned back around he saw that she had curled herself up in his armchair and fallen asleep. He put a blanket over her and turned out the light.

He didn't sleep however. He sat on the patio as the sun rose, trying to figure out what to do. He called James, and asked that he send over his granddaughter, Evelyn. Evelyn was taking a semester off from The Sorbonne and spent most days on the beach. She had been in and out of schools as a teenager—not a troublemaker but rather perpetually bored. James asked why, but Eli didn't say, just again insisted that it was urgent.

When Asma awoke, he made her oatmeal and was able to take a good look at her in the light. It was worse than he had imagined.

When the doorbell rang, Asma jumped. Eli put his hands out to communicate that it was okay.

When he opened the door, he was surprised to see both Evelyn and James standing there. From his panicked voice on their phone call, James had wanted to know what was going on, why Eli would suddenly need an unskilled twenty-year-old college student. Eli wasn't embarrassed or ashamed, but he hadn't intended to involve James in this.

Eli sighed and let them follow him into the kitchen, where Asma sat wide-eyed, staring at them.

"What the hell?" James said.

"She is the rabbit," Eli said.

"Excuse me?"

"The rabbit stealing from my garden. It wasn't a rabbit. It was her."

"So call the police," James quipped.

Evelyn had already become taken with the small child and had sat down next to her to introduce herself. Eli knew, for all Evelyn's wild child ways, she had a soft heart, which is why he'd wanted her to come round. She stayed smiling as she responded to her grandfather. "Can't you see? She is terrified."

James grabbed Eli by the elbow and pulled him into the next room. "So what do you intend to do with her?"

"Well, she is an orphan, or sort of. I think her father is in London. Maybe?"

James looked at his friend as if he had lost his mind. "Again, what do you intend to do with her?"

"I thought she could stay here while I tried to find her father."

"My friend, you cannot. This is insane. I have heard about this."

"Heard about what?"

"The children—they pretend to be orphans, then

some well-meaning family takes them in and then an uncle or father or brother shows up and says you've kidnapped the child. Then, unless you pay a huge sum, they will go to the police and claim you took them and god knows what else."

"But she is really alone. I went to the camp."

"You did what? Do you know the kind of people who live in that camp?"

"I lived in two camps as child," Eli said as he pushed past James and rejoined Evelyn and Asma in the kitchen. James had vaguely known the story, but it was something Eli rarely spoke of.

James also returned to the kitchen, but stood with his arms crossed as Eli explained the story to Evelyn. He asked her to stay with Asma until they could either locate her family or until the camp was closed. It was mere days, he knew. Then, he turned to James as he said the last part. "If they close the camp and I cannot locate any family, I will turn her over to child protection."

Evelyn smiled and said that it was a lovely plan and she hoped that Eli was right. She asked what he already knew about the girl's family, to which he handed her the postcard.

James stormed out then, urging Evelyn to do the same, but she didn't move. Eli said that Asma was in desperate need of a bath. Evelyn smiled and nodded her agreement.

"But what will we put her in?" Evelyn asked.

"Oh.." Eli hadn't thought of that. "Let me run into town."

James was surprised to see him come outside, but Eli moved right past him to his car. James knew that Eli never took his car. He knocked on the window.

"Where are you going?"

"Town. Evelyn is going to give her a bath but she cannot be redressed in those filthy clothes."

James got in the car and they headed into town. For a while he sat silently, until he could hold it in no longer.

"Seriously, my friend, I am not sure you have thought this through."

Eli was growing impatient with James. "What is there to think through? She is a small, scared, dirty, hungry child."

"And how dare you drag my Evie into this."

"She is a grown woman. She could have left."

"She has always been too soft hearted... I remember when she was about that same age."

Eli could tell his friend was relenting. He knew that when James looked at Asma, he could see his own granddaughter. Still, admitting defeat came easy for no man.

James hardly waited until the car had stopped before getting out, making a point to slam the door. Eli let out a heavy sigh and turned to his friend. "Do you know anything about buying clothes for children?"

James finally softened. "Come on, I will help." He knew there would be no pulling either Eli or Evelyn back from this, so he might as well.

***

Asma liked Evelyn immediately. She had soft features and bright eyes. After an impromptu game of hide and seek, Evelyn coaxed Asma into the bathroom. As Evelyn drew the bath, Asma was nervous, but then she put her hands in the warm water and Evelyn gestured for her to get in. Asma couldn't remember the last time she had taken a bath. Fatima did what she could, but usually it was just a bucket of cold water. Evelyn made bubbles, which made her smile. Once the bath had filled, Asma nervously got undressed. Seeing her discomfort, Evelyn made a show of covering her eyes.

The warm water felt delightful to Asma. She took turns blowing bubbles at Evelyn. Between the two of them, they had made the bathroom a mess. The water had turned a grimy color— the mark that the dirt left around the tub would take some scrubbing later —but still Asma never wanted to leave. Evelyn gave her the time to play before washing her hair and doing what she could to scrub her clean. Getting the knots out of her hair was too much of a challenge, but she was pleased to see no lice though. When the water turned cool, Evelyn urged her to scoot back so she could open the tap and add in more piping hot water. In truth, Evelyn was trying to delay until Eli got back; she didn't want Asma to have to wait around in only a towel. But when the hot water was depleted, he was still not back from town, so she found what she could for her to wear: an old T-shirt of Eli's. Asma wore it like gown, and smelled it repeatedly.

When James and Eli returned, Evelyn laughed at the hodgepodge of clothing that the two men had bought. She should have thought better than to let two octogenarian men pick out a little girl's clothes. She found that they had purchased three sizes of everything, and two dresses which were more suited to be worn at Easter than for every day.

Evelyn sighed, but was pleased to see some leggings and a shirt or two, none of which matched, but Asma didn't care. When she was dressed, she twirled around as if she had been dressed in ermine. Eli nodded and smiled. Asma beamed. James nodded approval as well, but Asma gave him only a grimace which caused laughter from Evie and Eli.

"That address is not a house. It's a hospital," Evelyn whispered to Eli, though she wasn't sure why, because she knew that Asma couldn't understand French.

"What?"

"On the postcard. I looked it up on my phone. It's not a house, it's a hospital. If her father was there…" Evie let her words drift off.

Eli suddenly—and for the first time—felt foolish. It didn't help that James stared at him with an I-told-you-so look. He looked over at Asma who was playing with Louise, dangling the stuffed toy by her ears and making her dance. She sat down in front of Chaya's painting, and Eli knew then that even if he was an old fool, he wasn't willing to give up yet.

Evie and Eli tried to coax a last name out of Asma. Each pointing to themselves and saying their full names: "Eli Bronstein," "Evelyn Richelle" and they would point to Asma and she would smile and say "Asma." This game went on until James threw his hands up and declared it useless.

Eli and Evie went back and forth on options. They could take her back to the camp and see if anyone knew anything more, but there would still be the language barrier. Eli wondered if the woman who had been passing out water the day before could translate, but then again, she hadn't been that helpful the first time. They listed the pros and cons, but ended at the same impasse they had started at.

"You know, she is very quiet," Evelyn observed after lunch. Eli had dug out some buckets and a few small shovels and the three adults were now sitting on the patio watching Asma dig in the sand.

"It can happen to children who have been traumatized. I remember thinking that Chaya was mute." Eli let out a little chuckle.

"You do know we will most likely have to turn her over to child services," Evie said sadly.

"I know."

Eli's mind couldn't help but drift back to Vera, and Yossi, and Sabine and the GIs with the chocolate—moments that had stayed with him for a lifetime. Even if they had to turn her over, at least she would have one or two happy days by the beach.

***

Eli cleared his throat. It was everything they had hoped for, but now he was suddenly very nervous; the double rings of the phone mirrored his own heartbeat.

It had all happened by chance, and it was a long shot, but anything was better than nothing—or at least that was what Eli kept reminding himself. Evie had been playing yet another round of hide and seek with Asma when Asma found Eli's stethoscope. Evie didn't think Eli would mind but still asked him if it was alright for her to play with it. Eli didn't mind. He had forgotten why it was even left lying about.

Asma expertly put it on and checked Louise for a heartbeat, then proceeded to check Evie and Eli.

James invited her to check his heart, but Asma declined. Eli told her that she would make a fine doctor one day.

"Baba doctor."

Eli nearly jumped out of his own skin. "Baba Doctor?" he asked again.

Asma nodded.

Evie and James had yet to figure out what was transpiring, when Eli asked who had the postcard. Evie had left it on the kitchen table that afternoon, and she handed it to Eli. They had attempted to call, but their asking whether the hospital had any Syrian patients was as futile as they knew it would be. The receptionist had been kind but explained that she couldn't give out any information on past or current patients.

"Baba Doctor here?" Eli said pointing to postcard. Asma again nodded.

Evie and James stared at him dumbfounded. Eli caught his breath. "She is saying her dad is a doctor. We assumed that, because the postcard came from a hospital, he was a patient, but she is telling us he is a doctor. Evie, can you pull up that website again for the hospital?"

"Sure." Eli hovered as she moved swiftly on his laptop, which had, before now, only been collecting dust.

"Here," she said, turning it around to face Eli.

"Is there a list of doctors? Maybe there will be pictures and she could point him out."

James interjected to tell Eli what his own better judgement was already saying. "Don't get too far ahead of yourself."

Evie clicked a few times, but shook her head. "There is a list, but no pictures."

"Any of them sound middle eastern?"

"There is a Dr. Farhad Behzadi or a Dr. Ahmed Bahar"

Asma came running when she heard the second name and with that, Eli was convinced they had found him.

"Sounds like a very common name," James added to no one in particular.

Eli looked at his watch. It was already eight at night. Still, he called the hospital, but was informed that Dr. Bahar wouldn't be in until the following morning. The woman asked if Eli wanted to leave a message, to which Eli only asked that he please call him first thing in the morning, and he left his name as Dr. Elijah Bronstein. The woman seemed surprised that the callback number was in France, but took it down all the same. James sighed and went home, but assured everyone he would be back tomorrow.

That night, despite not hardly sleeping the night before, Eli still couldn't settle. Earlier, he had tip-toed through the house to check on Asma, who was sleeping on a pile of down feather comforters, and Evie, who was asleep, but contorted on the couch. Both were sound asleep, so Eli returned to his room.

As soon as he woke up, Eli immediately dialed the hospital. He was still rubbing the sleep out of his eyes when the receptionist informed him that Dr. Bahar was not in yet. When Eli called a few hours later, he was told the doctor was in surgery. Eli stressed once more that it was extremely urgent.

Finally, late in the afternoon, the receptionist said the words that sent a cold chill through Eli. "Yes, he said he was expecting your call. Let me connect you."

"This is Dr. Bahar speaking," the man said coolly.

"Yes, right. This is Dr. Elijah Bronstein."

"My receptionist said you have been looking for me. I apologize that I could not return your call earlier. What kind of medicine do you practice?"

"I was an ophthalmologist, but I have been retired for some time."

For the first time, Ahmed noticed how old Eli sounded, and the confusion in his voice was palpable. "And what can I do for a retired ophthalmologist?"

Eli struggled to figure out what he was going to say next. "It's about your daughter."

"I think you have me mistaken with someone else."

"We found a postcard," he continued, hoping that the man wouldn't hang up. "Her name is Asma. We are in Calais. She doesn't say much. I am sorry if this is the wrong person. She has been stealing from my garden."

It felt like an eternity passed, as the silence hung in the air.

"Hello?" Eli asked, unsure if the man had hung up or walked away.

"Is this some kind of sick joke?" Ahmed asked.

"No."

"Can I speak to her?"

"Of course." Eli called Asma, and Ahmed could feel the room spin around him. It was not possible.

"Asma?" Ahmed asked, but she didn't respond. He could hear her breathing. He also heard Eli and a female voice in the background, urging her to say hello. Still, it was silent. Asma thought the man sounded like her father, but at the same time, he also sounded like Saad, so she didn't utter a word.

"I am sorry," Eli said as he rejoined the call after a few minutes.

Ahmed had convinced himself that this was some type of scam, and was about to end the call when he heard Asma laugh in the background. "Where can I met you? I can be there in two hours."

Ahmed was already shoving work papers into his bag, and then told himself he didn't need his papers.

"The ride from London to Calais takes three hours," Eli said.

"I will be on the next train. Here is my cell phone number."

Ahmed recited his number and then hung up the phone. He immediately called Grace. He told her what had just happened, that a man had found his daughter in France and that he was going to get her. Grace connected in her husband and asked Ahmed to repeat the story. George, who was already at the hospital, listened as Ahmed frantically filled them in.

As delicately as either could muster, both told Ahmed that it couldn't be true. He couldn't be sure that it was his child just based on its laugh. Ahmed knew it was her laugh. It was the same laugh as Safia's; he would always recognize it.

When their common sense wouldn't persuade him, and their attempts to temper his mood failed, George and Grace stepped into action. At first, they debated the fastest route, train or tunnel, and eventually decided on train. If this did turn out to be a hoax, a public setting like a train station would be best. Grace offered to go to Ahmed's house and get any travel documents for Asma, though she still didn't believe it was true. In the meantime, George made sure that all of Ahmed's surgeries were rescheduled, and drove him to St Pancras International. When they arrived, Ahmed turned to thank his friend for the ride, but George parked the car and got out with him, saying that he had also cleared his surgery schedule for the day.

Grace was already there and holding three tickets. Ahmed vibrated with excitement. George and Grace eyed each other nervously.

Ahmed called Eli to advise him that they would be arriving at Calais Ville at four in the afternoon. Eli said he would meet them on the platform, even if he was not sure who Ahmed meant by "we."

"What if it is not him?" Evie asked.

"What do you mean?"

"What if it's not her father?"

"I don't think a doctor would leave London at the spur of the moment to come for a child that is not his."

"Fine!" Evie said, still unconvinced. "But I am not even attempting to tell Asma anything."

Hours passed, that felt like an eternity for all parties. Evie patiently worked the knots from Asma's hair while they waited, braiding it into two pigtails. She smiled, but Asma could sense the energy had shifted and was becoming nervous, although she did not know why. Evie was going to put her in one of the dresses that James and Eli had bought, but then thought better of it. If this man was her father, he would be able to spot her without a fancy dress. When the time came to leave for the station, Asma began crying. She knew she was going somewhere, but she didn't know where, and she didn't want to leave the lovely cottage by the beach or leave the kind people. She clung to Louise as she was talked into the car.

On the train, George and Grace tried to make small talk, but it was useless. Grace in particular had a very bad feeling about this, and insisted that if Asma wasn't at the station they would, under no circumstances, go anywhere else.

All Grace and George's doubts seeped into Ahmed's mind, but even as man of science, this was one time where his brain would not overrule his heart.

On the platform, Asma held Eli's hand with one hand and Louise with the other. As the train pulled in and sea of people emerged, she clung to them tighter. As impatient travelers pushed their way through, Eli moved Asma in front of him to keep her from getting trampled. He placed both hands on her shoulders to try to reassure her that everything was okay.

Ahmed pushed past people to disembark. George and Grace struggled to keep up with him in a flurry of "excuse mes" and "sorrys" as they followed him onto the platform. But, ahead of them, Ahmed froze. He could see nothing, but the hundred or so others who were making their way into the station.

"Baba!" Asma shouted and burst forward, tearing her way down the platform.

Ahmed heard it, but still couldn't see her until she called out again.

"Baba!"

She jumped into his arms, and he wrapped her so tight, neither could breathe for a moment. Grace was sobbing, as was Evie. Ahmed must have embraced her longer than he thought, because when he looked up, the platform was completely clear of people, except for George, Grace, two elderly gentlemen and a young woman.

Introductions were made but few words were exchanged. In both the best and worst times, there are simply no good words. Ahmed asked Asma about her mother and brother, but she shook her head, and Ahmed knew what he had already known.

Ahmed laughed when Evie asked to see Asma's passport, but was thankful for her in the same breathe. He knew immediately that it was neither Eli nor James who had braided her hair. Ahmed offered Eli money for any expenses, but Eli wouldn't hear of it.

"Can I buy you lunch or dinner?" Ahmed offered, but Eli declined, insisting that he had been neglecting a chess game that he had to return to. Moreover, Eli couldn't say it, but he didn't want to be thanked.

Evie said goodbye and Asma hugged her. James shook Asma's tiny hand.

Eli knelt to say goodbye, his knees protesting as he bent down, and he knew he would need help to return to standing. He asked Ahmed if he would translate.

"Goodbye, Asma. I am glad we found your Baba. Do me a favor, okay? Look after Louise. She was a very good friend to me for a very long time."

Asma nodded and gave Eli a big hug, then George and Grace helped him back to his feet.

And he turned to leave. Eli looked back one last time to see Asma holding on to Ahmed, Louise still dangling by an ear. He laughed to himself, thinking about the stories that stuffed bunny could tell, but he hoped that it would be the last one like this.

Printed in Great Britain
by Amazon